Average Boy's Above-Average Year

ADVENTURES OF

Average Boy's
Above-Average Year

Bob Smiley

A Focus on the Family Resource
Published by Tyndale House Publishers

Cover design by Michael Harrigan

Illustrations by David Harrington

For information about special discounts for bulk purchases, please contact Tyndale House Publishers at csresponse@tyndale.com, or call 1-855-277-9400.

ISBN 978-1-64607-058-9

Printed in the United States of America

28	27	26	25	24	23	22
7	6	5	4	3	2	1

Chapter 1

I want to get one thing straight. I'm Average Boy. I am not a wimpy kid. Just ask anyone. Well, you aren't supposed to talk to strangers, so don't ask them. And don't ask Donny because he doesn't like me right now.

You could ask my dog. He knows me pretty well. But he has a very limited vocabulary, so you won't get very far. (That's another reason not to ask Donny. Limited vocabulary.)

I'm not wimpy. Not at all. I play all kinds of sports right up until I'm asked to stop, usually by coaches. And I'm not nervous about starting middle school. You'd think I would be, because it's a new place with waaay bigger kids. I've heard some of the boys shave.

That's another reason not to trust Donny. He's been held back so much he's already shaving. Donny loves to scare other students by flexing his muscles . . . or growing a beard.

Nope, I'm not nervous. I think middle school will be great. There are so many different sports! Sports are like a religion here in Texas, especially football. I don't know what it's like in other countries, but in Texas football is worshipped. People here can't recall Jesus' twelve disciples, but they can rattle off the starting offensive and defensive lines for the Dallas Cowboys.

I wonder if Jesus and His buddies ever played football. Jesus could've been the best player. He could just divide the other team like Moses parting the Red Sea and run for a touchdown every time. Plus, He could heal anyone who got injured.

I've already signed up to wrestle for my school this year. I watch wrestling on TV and can't wait to do it on a team. My mom made me the coolest cape and mask to wear at matches. I'm going to call myself "The Smiley Slammer." I've even picked out the intro music for the coach to play when I walk onto the mat.

It's going to be awesome! I've been perfecting my wrestling maneuvers all week. My dog won't come to me anymore—but that just means I'm doing it right. Oh, that's another reason you shouldn't ask my dog about me. Like Donny, he's pretty mad at me right now.

Anyway, I'm constantly practicing my moves. In fact, I'm standing on the picnic table right now, waiting for my dog to walk by. Once he's in range, I'm going to attempt an atomic body smash.

Okay, atomic may be too strong a word. I'm barely fifty pounds, which means I'll be wrestling in the lightest weight class. Instead of smashing opponents, I'll probably just float down on them like a feather. I wonder if you can tickle an opponent into submission. I've never seen that on TV. But I tend to do things differently than other kids.

I'm also excited about wrestling because I get to wear a mask. I have it on right now. Mom says I look better this way. This is probably my fault. Last week, I put some sun-highlighter spray in my hair. Instead of giving me highlights, like the package advertised, it turned my hair white.

Dad says I now look like a Q-tip. That's not a good look for a new middle school student. I either need to bulk up my body or dye my hair back to its normal color. Anyway, if my hair still looks this way in a week or two, maybe I'll change my wrestling name to "The Blonde Bobber."

Anyhow, you probably have some questions about me. I get a lot of questions from people. The question I'm asked most often is, "Why are you in our pool?"

That's an easy one. My neighbors don't have a lock on their fence. The second most asked question I get is, "How did you get the name Average Boy?"

The name actually fits. You see, I'm not really good at anything. When I was in elementary school, I entered a long-distance race. It might have been a marathon, or something even harder. I think it was called a 5K.

My dad was a runner, so he was excited to watch me. Once the race started, he drove to the finish line to wait. And wait. I still remember when I saw him cheering for me. Everyone else had already gone home after the ribbons were awarded, but Dad stayed until I finished the race.

As I crossed the finish line, he shouted, "Wow, that was some truly average running!"

Dad is often encouraging like that. He's always truthful too.

Don't feel sorry for me. I like being average. In fact, C is my favorite grade in school. C means average. But I like to think that C also stands for Christian. Because God is present in my life, He can take my average ability and do great things with it. So rather than living up to my "average" name, I want to honor God's name. So that's what makes me Average Boy, superhero for hire. Mostly to mow lawns.

That's enough about me. I need to concentrate. My dog just came up from the creek. It's time to get back to wrestling practice. Here comes the atomic body smash! I know I can master this move, because my mask already feels atomic. It's fusing to my face in this hot Texas sun.

My heartbeat quickens as my dog shakes the water from his coat. For non-dog owners, a coat is his fur. I don't want anyone to think we're rich and that my dog wears a nice leather jacket.

Feeling mostly dry, my dog bounds for the house. His
tongue is sticking out of his mouth. I'm not sure if it's
directed at me, but it's go time. I crouch down like the
wrestlers I've seen on TV. My dog nears the table. I'm
ready to spring. . . .

"Bob, get off that table!" Mom yells.

Noooo! I shout, in my head. I've learned from experience not to shout at my mom with my actual voice.

My dog runs off. I've never seen professional wrestlers
get their signature move messed up by their moms, but
I'm sure it happens.

Oh well, I've got two more days to practice before
school starts.

I peel the wrestling mask from my face, feeling like a
human banana.

"Why don't you do something useful?" Mom says.

"I was trying to," I reply.

"Attacking our dog isn't useful," Mom says. "He's been
frazzled since your brother tried to ride him."

Mom makes a good point, even though that homemade rodeo was fun. Maybe I can be more useful at a
neighbor's house. Mr. Polvado down the street does have a
dog. I could practice on him. (The dog, not Mr. Polvado.)

Mr. Polvado is somewhere around 183 years old. His
house is filled with history. One day I saw him talking on
something he called a "landline." I know this sounds made

up, but a landline is actually a big phone connected to his house with a cord! I don't know how he listens to music when he goes for a walk. Maybe he has a really long cord?

Anyway, Mr. Polvado loves when I drop by. His house is a short bike ride away. I park in his driveway and knock on the door.

"Why are you here?" he greets me warmly.

"I came to hang out," I say. "What are you doing?"

"I was listening to the quiet, but I can see now that it's over. I thought you were in school?"

"Nope! Not for two more days."

"Hmmm . . . I guess your school didn't get my email to start sooner."

"That's funny," I say. "Do you even have email?"

"You caught me. I heard someone talk about it on TV."

"Did you ever wrestle?" I ask. "You know with dinosaurs or something."

Mr. Polvado has a funny way of laughing. It sounds like a groan.

"I'm going to wrestle for my school this year," I explain. "I'm practicing on my dog. Hey, where's your dog?"

"I think he smelled you coming and is hiding somewhere," Mr. Polvado says.

"That's just my wrestling mask," I say. "It gets hot in there."

Mr. Polvado asks if I want some cookies. Ten minutes

later he returns with a plateful of crackers. I've always thought he had a strange sense of humor.

"Are you ready to start middle school?" Mr. Polvado asks.

I've been asking myself that question all summer. And yes, I'm ready! I can't wait for this school year to start! Last week, my youth pastor encouraged everyone to focus on taking more risks this year. Not dumb risks like trying to eat a bowl of hair. No, he wants us to take real risks that push us out of our comfort zones, make us try new things, and help reveal God's love to others. That's what I plan to do.

And to make it interesting, he said whoever pushes themselves to do the most and keeps track of these decisions in a journal would win a new GameStation 6.5 video game console. I couldn't believe it! The Gamestation 6.5 is way better than the 6.0. And by way better, I mean by .5. I can already feel the controller in my hands.

Can I win it? Well, it just so happens that one of my superpowers, in addition to peeling off stuck wrestling masks, is trying new things, taking risks, and getting outside of my comfort zone. And now I have another reason to do those things this year!

So I think middle school is going to be great. Look out, world! It's time for Average Boy's above-average year!

Chapter 2

Okay. Here I go. Once I walk through those big glass doors, I will officially be a middle schooler . . . practically a grown-up. First, I need to pull out my phone and check my mustache. Cool. It looks great.

I drew it on early this morning, using my mom's eyebrow pencil, but I don't think other kids will notice it's fake. I drew it on very lightly. And then Mom thought I had leftover breakfast on my lip and kept trying to rub it off as she drove me to school.

I can't believe I'm so nervous. I also can't believe my mom is taking a photo of me outside by the school sign. Is there some kind of class for moms that teaches them how to embarrass their kids? If so, my mom probably made straight A's.

Sarah walks by laughing as Mom snaps my photo. I tell her we're doing a photoshoot for a project I'm working on.

"Is it one of those before-and-after pictures where guys get super muscular?" she asks. "You're the perfect 'before' shape."

Did you hear that? Sarah thinks I'm about to get super muscular.

Anyway, it's time. Time to make new friends, time to try new things, and time to have a better than average year. I rush forward to meet as many new people as I can.

Bad idea. Well, the rushing into school was fine, but forgetting that the big glass doors were closed was not. I smacked right into them. But I did meet someone new. Mrs. Black is the school nurse. I met her when I woke up a few minutes ago.

"You'll be fine," Mrs. Black tells me. "But you may want to have your nose checked out."

"Oh, it looked like that before I hit the door," I say.

Yeah, my nose is a little crooked. If I obeyed the phrase, "Follow your nose," I would walk in a circle.

"Well, at least have the bruising on your upper lip looked at," Mrs. Black adds.

Yea! *Someone noticed my mustache.*

I glance at my phone and realize I'm about to be late for class.

"Thanks, I'm sure I'll be seeing lots of you this year," I say. "But I've got to go now. I want to make a good first impression on my math teacher."

I speed walk down the hall, holding my hand in front of me in case the school has any more invisible doors. I'm not that good at football, but I'm guessing this is what a running back feels like. Well, a skinny running back without pads. Still, it's important to be safe . . . and on time.

I'm two minutes late. I walk in right as the teacher says her name. "Good morning class. I'm Mrs. Villin."

Everyone turns to stare at me. All their eyes make me even more nervous, so I do what any other average kid would do: I break into a freestyle rap.

"Hi, Mrs. Villin, I'm chillin', ready to be killin', in class, so brass, sorry I'm late, but I have a hall pass!"

For being on the spot, I thought it was a pretty good rhyme. Evidently, Mrs. Villin doesn't like rap music.

"Please sit down and stop interrupting class," she says.

Oh well, I did make an impression. I just didn't achieve the "good" part. I reach into my backpack, hand her a piece of paper, and head to a seat in the back of the classroom.

I settle into my seat and open my backpack. That's when I realize I didn't give Mrs. Villin a hall pass. I gave her lyrics to my new song, "Bob Is the Best." Not only am

I an amazing freestyle rap artist, I'm part of a band. We call ourselves the Barn Boys, probably because we practice in a barn. I jump up to give her the real hall pass, but she tells me to sit down.

"You can give me your hall pass after class," Mrs. Villin says with a smile. "And you have all year to prove to me that your song title is true."

I sit back down. My plan to try new things is working . . . just not the way I thought it would. I try to listen. My brain races. Dad says my brain moves much faster than my legs.

I look at my schedule. History class is next. History is in my future! "Ha!" I blurt out loud, laughing at my own joke. My humor is lost on the rest of the class.

"Please be quiet, Mr. Smiley," Mrs. Villin says.

I hope Mrs. Villin doesn't turn out to be a *real* villain. I don't think she will. There's something about her that I like.

Class is over! At least I think it's over. Billy just woke me up. He's been my best friend since third grade. I look around. The other kids are grabbing their backpacks, so it really is time to go. I grab my stuff and catch up with Billy, and we walk to history together. I think I need more sleep at night.

Even if Mrs. Villin isn't a villain, Mr. Garner might be. He starts our first history class by giving us a test! This is going to be a hard class.

Don't adults know that students use summer to delete our brains of school knowledge and make room for more important stuff like video game maps and song lyrics? Then, in the fall, we fill it back up with school stuff. It's a perfect, time-honored system that shouldn't be messed with. But Mr. Garner says he wants to see how much we know before he starts teaching us.

I actually know the first couple of questions: Name the first president of the United States. *Easy.* Abraham Lincoln. Next to Lincoln's name, I write down that he also invented the lightbulb in hopes of getting extra credit. I bet Abe did that so he could see what was in his refrigerator.

The next question is about the Civil War. Mom always tells me and my brother to be civil. She explained that means to be courteous and polite. So next to the question "Who fought the Civil War?" I write: "There can't be something called a civil war."

You'd think a teacher would know that those two words go against each other. Just like you can't have "broccoli dessert," "vacation homework," or "jumbo shrimp," it's impossible to have a "civil war."

The rest of the questions are pretty easy like that, so I'm one of the first ones finished. I walk my paper to Mr. Garner's desk. He glances at my answers and says I only got one question right.

"Well, at least I remembered my name correctly," I joke.

Mr. Garner laughs. It's odd, because it sort of sounds like Mr. Polvado's groaning laugh. "I can tell you're a jokester, pointing out that oxymoron about the Civil War," he says. "We'll be learning about another one, too, this year—the Great Depression."

Did he just call me an oxymoron? I'm not the smartest kid, but I'm not an oxymoron either.

"I might not have done well on this test, but I want this year to be the best one yet!" I say. "No offense, Mr. Garner, but I'm focused on the *future*, not history."

"Ah, then you do need history," he says. "Because those who don't learn from the past are destined to repeat it. If you want a good future, you need to learn from history's mistakes."

I've never thought about that. But he's right. I've definitely learned lessons in the past that have helped me later in life. For instance, I'll never put a stray kitten in my backpack again without first checking to see if it's a baby skunk. I also know there's no such thing as an albino apple, and I'll never trust Clint again when he offers me food. (That was the worst tasting onion I've ever eaten.)

So history does teach us things. Hmmm, I'm actually pretty excited about history class now. Maybe Mr. Garner does have a lot to teach us, or at least me.

The bell rings. History is now in the past. *Hakuna ah-bye-bye.* Whoever said middle school was the worst years of his life was totally wrong.

Hey, I forgot to get my song lyrics back from Mrs. Villin. Better swing by sometime today. It'll be thrillin' to see her again.

Chapter 3

I'm at lunch now.

The rest of my morning classes went well. I learned in science that we aren't allowed to turn on the Bunsen burners without permission. I also discovered that my backpack is made out of nylon . . . and nylon melts.

My fourth period class ended up getting changed. I was signed up for choir because I love singing. But after my first solo, my choir teacher said she thought I'd be good at band. I guess my band talent outshines all my other talents, even singing. My choir teacher discovered this when

I burst out singing while slapping my leg to keep rhythm. My choir teacher stopped calling attendance.

"Why are you singing?" she asked. "And is that your real voice?"

"I've been blessed with perfect pitch," I said.

"Well, I'm going to hit that pitch to band class," she told me.

Can you believe that? It's only the first day, and I've already received two hall passes!

Mrs. Brown, the band teacher, was a bit confused when I walked in. I decided to sing to her about what happened. You know, like they do in musical movies to explain the plot.

"I've got a hall pass in my hand, and I've been transferred to band. I could learn the saxophone or maybe the trombone. Just tell me what to play. I'll grab an instrument and make your day."

I hate to toot my own horn, but my rhyming skills are on point today.

After I finished my song, Mrs. Brown said it made perfect sense why I was sent to band. I guess she saw my hand tapping rhythm as well. She tried me out on several instruments and finally decided I'd be good at the triangle.

Instantly, I became third chair triangle player. This was confusing because no one else plays the triangle, and I didn't see two other chairs near me. I guess I have a lot to learn about band. But that's what school is about, learning new stuff.

And right now I'm learning I have no place to sit.

Lunch was actually the biggest thing I worried about. Billy has A lunch. It's probably the only A he'll get in school this year. And I have B lunch, which apparently comes *after* A lunch. This means I'm not sure who to sit with.

I see Donny at an empty table by himself. I'm not feeling that brave. He's still holding a grudge, and today his beard looks especially intimidating.

My fake mustache has now worn off because I've been sweating. I guess that's fine because everyone kept asking me how I bruised my lip.

"You need to sit down," the lunch monitor says to me. "If you don't start eating soon, your ice cream will become soup and then the soup will become yogurt. And nobody likes yogurt."

I laugh at her joke and scan more tables. I decide to do something that would make my youth pastor proud. I'm going to take a risk. I spot three kids that I've never seen before. I walk over and try to make some new friends.

"Hi, I'm Bob, but you can call me Average Boy," I say. "Can I sit down?"

They look at me like most kids do: strangely.

I sit down and learn that the three kids are named Jordan, Mark, and Luke. Wow, those names are right from the Bible! Last night my dad reminded me that picking good friends at school is super important. He told me that friends can influence my thoughts and shape my actions. "So choose wisely and pick godly friends at school," he said.

Well, I say you can't get more godly than Jordan, Mark, and Luke. Well, maybe Jesus, Paul, or Moses. Or maybe Ishbi-benob. Still, Jordan, Mark, and Luke are pretty good.

Anyway, I tell them a few jokes and show them my cool new colored pencil set I got for art class.

"Can I have the red pencil?" Jordan asks.

"That's the best one," I say. "Plus, I don't want to break up the set. I have art later so I need all of them. Would you like some ice cream soup instead?"

"Nah," Jordan says. "Looks too much like yogurt. How about you just give me that red pencil?"

"I can't. I mean, what if I have to draw an orange with a sunburn?"

"Okay," he says. "We'll see."

I don't know what he means by that, but at least he doesn't seem mad. In fact, Mark starts telling some jokes. I guess his name wasn't taken from the Bible. He doesn't seem to be a Christian, judging from the punchlines. Maybe I can get him to start going to church with me. That could really help me win the video game console.

I wish lunch could go longer. I was worried, but now

I have three new friends that I can invite to church. They even watch my backpack while I go to the bathroom. Trust is a big key when picking out friends.

"See you guys tomorrow," I say when the bell rings.

I sling my backpack over my shoulder and race walk to English. I've stopped sticking out one of my arms because everyone was calling me "Heisman." I don't get it. I'm not choking; I don't need the Heisman Maneuver. I'm just trying to be safe.

I walk into class early. Because this class is all about reading and writing, I start reading aloud everything the teacher has written on the board. Again, it's important to make a great first impression. I want her to know that I can read really well. She thanks me by saying, "That's all the reading you need to do today. Please take a seat."

Once everyone is seated, she passes out a book that we all need to read before Christmas break. It's not long, so I put it in my backpack. Then I start thinking about all the different presents I want for Christmas. Before I know it, class is over.

And then it's time for art class. Our teacher is named Mr. Quick. He told us the first thing we'll do every day is draw whatever word he has on the board. He calls it "The Quick Draw." It sounds like art is going to be a blast!

The word on the board is fireplace. Good thing I didn't give away my red pencil.

I reach into my backpack to grab my colored pencils. Hmm. I can't find them. I know I had them in my backpack at lunch right before I went to the bathroom.

Oh no.

Chapter 4

Yes, I've been wrong in the past. I was wrong about thinking that strawberry shampoo might taste like strawberries. I was wrong about that squirrel in our backyard. Really wrong. He did *not* want a hug.

However, I don't think I've ever been as wrong as I was about Jordan, Mark, and Luke. They would not make good friends. In fact, I now refer to them as the "Terrible Threesome."

I'm a month into school, and those kids are the worst! Actually, getting that strawberry shampoo taste out of my mouth was the real worst. Even worse than that honey harvest shea butter hand cream that I once tried for breakfast.

The words "honey" and "butter" should never be put on a product, unless you're supposed to spread it on toast.

Sitting with the Terrible Threesome at lunch is definitely one of my all-time worst decisions. They stole the colored pencils out of my backpack when I went to the bathroom during lunch that first day. A few days later they put a rubber spider on my chair in math class when I got up to sharpen my pencil. That prank actually wasn't too embarrassing because the rest of the kids in class were impressed that I could jump so high.

Last week they pulled their biggest stunt on me. They glued my locker shut. Mark was standing right by it, so I should've known something was up. He said it was probably just stuck and I should pull really hard.

So I did, and everyone got a nice laugh when the locker door popped open and banged me in the face. I'm glad I can spread a little cheer.

I'm not the Terrible Threesome's only target. They pull pranks on everyone. Just yesterday, the Terrible Threesome tied Randy's shoelaces together when he fell asleep in history class. Randy tripped and fell when he stood up to leave.

Their pranks are getting more dangerous (especially for my head) and have to be stopped, so I'm going to confront those three the best way I know how.

I'm going to get Donny to do it.

Not that I'm afraid of them. Again, I'm not wimpy, just smart.

And I'll have to use my smarts to get Donny to help. I can't just ask him, because he's mad at me. Plus, he's huge. I have to use a ladder if I want to talk to him face-to-face. Donny used to be the biggest bully in elementary school. The biggest in size, I mean. One time my gym teacher had us run around Donny because our track was being remodeled.

Instead of asking Donny to confront Jordan, Mark, and Luke, I'm going to trick him into helping. And I know the perfect place to do this: the lunchroom.

Mark thinks it's really funny to throw food at people when the teachers aren't looking. There are two problems with this. The first problem is that by "people," I mean me. Mark only ever throws food at me. The second problem is the teachers never catch him. They just sit at their teacher table doing what all adults do—stare at their phones. (And they say it's the kids who have a problem.)

My plan is foolproof. I'm sitting two tables behind the Terrible Threesome but one table in front of Donny. Of course, I can't take all the credit for my plan. The lunch ladies did serve a side salad today.

Small tomatoes are a big temptation for Mark. And his plate is loaded with about thirty of them. I'm not worried. Well, I'm a little worried. I shouldn't have worn a white T-shirt today. And I need the last teacher to sit down and get on her phone.

Good. There she goes. Now everything is set.

Mark starts by throwing a tomato over his shoulder toward me. It plops in the middle of my food. I grab it, knowing my plan is about to start working.

"Nice warning shot," I whisper loud enough for him to hear.

He turns and fires the next tomato at my head, but misses completely. He hits my shoulder. Luke and Jordan laugh. They are facing me at their table.

"Come on," I urge him, "put some pepper on that tomato!"

Mark totally misses my joke because he sprinkles pepper on the next tomato he grabs.

"Here comes some pepper," he whispers back at me. Then he checks the teacher table to make sure they're still consumed with social media. They are. He turns around and hurls the tomato right at my head.

That's exactly what I'm waiting for! I duck and the tomato hits Donny in the back of the head. Splat! . . . Whimper.

The small whimpering sound, I assume, comes from the tomato hitting Donny's concrete block of a head.

Donny slams his hands on the table and turns around. I switch to my normal fighting stance, which is curling up on the floor. He looks at me and I point toward the Terrible Threesome. "I think Mark threw something at you," I say.

Donny stares at the Terrible Threesome. I can actually feel the heat coming off of Donny's forehead. He's really mad. God doesn't want us to lose our temper, but I sort of feel God would be okay with it this time. After all, I need protection, and this is part of my plan.

It's all going perfectly.

I've actually had lots of great ideas in the past. I invented a soda volcano that shot soda twelve feet into the air. And once I realized it needed to erupt outside of the house, my parents agreed. I also convinced my parents to open Christmas presents alphabetically. They could go by "Average Boy" or "Bob," and I'd still be the first one to open something.

The point is, I've had a lot of really good ideas. This isn't one of them.

Like I said earlier, I've been wrong about stuff in the past. And boy was I ever wrong about my "perfect plan" to get back at the Terrible Threesome.

Chapter 5

Donny storms over to Mark. For the first time ever, Mark looks nervous. I quickly uncurl and stand on my chair to get a better view. Donny leans into Mark's face, which means Donny has to bend completely over. The teachers all respond by continuing to click on their phones.

"Did you throw a tomato at me?" Donny asks.

"Me? Uh, well. I—" Mark starts to answer. Then he looks past Donny and sees me standing on my chair.

"No." Mark smiles. "I would never waste a tomato by throwing it at the biggest kid in school. Look, Average Boy has a tomato in his hand. He probably threw it."

Mark's words fade away as everyone in the lunchroom looks at me. I look down and see that the tomato that landed in my food is somehow still in my hand. This was not part of my plan. Neither was Donny turning around and walking back toward me. I have to do something quick.

"Facebook is giving away free shoes to teachers!" I shout.

All the teachers look up. Donny freezes in his tracks.

"Mr. Smiley, please sit down," Mr. Garner tells me. "And have your fathe—wait that's Donny. Donny, go back to your lunch, too."

"This isn't over," Donny whispers through gritted teeth.

A week has passed since the lunchroom showdown and things haven't gotten any better. I once learned at church that God doesn't want us to take revenge on people. I should've stuck with that advice. Instead, I tried to get back at the Terrible Threesome by making Donny mad at them.

But now I have to dodge four people! So far I haven't run into Donny. But I must always be thinking ahead.

I'm currently hiding in Mr. Gribble's office. He's our janitor. You'd think a janitor's office would be the cleanest room in the building. It's not. It smells like mops and dirty gym socks. Those are two smells you'll never find in a jellybean flavor or in a scented candle.

Donny is out in the hallway.

"Have you seen Average Boy?" I hear him ask.

"You might want to check the weight room," someone says. And by "someone," I mean Sarah.

"Why would he be in the weight room?" Donny says.

"Have you seen his arms?" Sarah replies. "He needs to be in the weight room."

Okay. I'm grateful Sarah is protecting me, but her comment hurts. My arms aren't that skinny. Sarah knows I'm in Mr. Gribble's office. Right before I ducked in here, she asked what I was doing. Hang on, I hear them talking some more.

"No! Donny! Don't go in the janitor's office!" Sarah says in a loud voice.

I quickly try to hide behind a mop handle as the door bursts open.

"BOO!" a scary voice says.

I fall back into a stack of mops.

"You're not funny!" I shout out.

Sarah doesn't say anything back. She's too busy laughing.

I stand up and peer down the hallway.

"Donny's not here," she says. "He went to the weight room. But you should've seen your face. Hilarious!"

Some people just don't understand true comedy.

After surviving the week with some help from my friends, I get to go to church. They say there's safety in numbers. That's why I love youth group. Everyone here shares the same beliefs and values. They'd never let Mark throw a tomato at me or glue me to my chair in math class.

Oh yeah, that happened, too. What is it with the Terrible Threesome and glue?

Our youth pastor is teaching from the book of Acts. He talks about how Peter stepped out of his comfort zone to tell people about God's love. It wasn't easy. Our youth pastor wants us to do the same. I tried that earlier in the week. I guess I picked the wrong kids.

"Anyone have a story about how they took a risk for God?" our youth pastor asks.

Nothing is more risky than getting the biggest kid at school mad at you, but I'm pretty sure that's not what he's talking about.

Oh, wow! Jenny told us about how she's trying to do something for homeless people. She's packed plastic bags full of granola bars, dried fruit, bottled water, Kleenex, and a mini-Bible. She put them in her mom's car. Now whenever they see a homeless person who's hungry, they give him or her a bag. Jenny called them "food and faith" bags.

So, this contest is on! Our youth pastor says we're going
to vote every week and keep track of who's standing up for
God the most. The person at the end of the year who gets
the greatest number of weekly votes will receive the new
game console.

I need to win this! The video game console I use right
now is called an Atari. My dad played on it when he was a
kid. I think he, George Washington, and Moses competed
against each other. The controller only has one button and
a huge joystick. How can you do anything fun with just
one button?

Jenny wins the vote for this week. But I'm great at coming from behind. That's because I'm usually behind. My
trick is to keep the same average pace until I win at the end.
I read a book about how that strategy worked for a turtle. It
hasn't worked for me yet, but I'm due for a victory.

And if I can win the GameStation 6.5, then everyone will want to come to my house. I'll be the cool kid. Of course, I'll need to buy some games, too, and they aren't cheap.

Once church is over and I get home, I run to my room and look in my backpack to see how much money I have saved. The first thing I see is the book from my reading and writing class. I didn't make the best first impression, but Mrs. Wordsmith has been great. I think she was born to teach English, just like my friend Clara Seawright would be a great eye doctor or my neighbor Mr. Kitchin would make a good chef. Anyway, I need to remember to start reading that book.

I find some homework that I forgot to turn in and an assignment that's due tomorrow. But no money.

The next depressing thing happens when I look in my wallet. It's empty. I know I had money last week, but I can't remember what I spent it on. Oh, here's a receipt in the pocket of the wallet.

Ahh . . . it looks like I bought a new wallet. I don't know why I did that. Why would I spend all my money on something that's supposed to hold all my money? That's like selling my bike to buy a new bike helmet.

"Lunch is ready," Mom shouts from downstairs.

Good, I think better with a full stomach. This afternoon I'm going to plan some good ways to make money.

I also need a plan to do more risky things for God. You can't always trust turtles, no matter how steady they race. I need something fast. I need to take the lead at youth group and then stay ahead.

Chapter 6

Making money is tough. That's what my dad always says.

I look up jobs online and read about some pretty good ones. From my research, being a CEO of a company is the best way to make lots of money. The problem is most big companies already have a CEO.

That's not fair, I think. *All the good jobs are already taken.*

I email Google to see if they have any positions that I'm qualified for. They email me back a few days later and tell me to contact them in ten years. That's ridiculous! If my plans go right, I won't even need a job in ten years. I'll be too busy flying on my private jet to my sold-out comedy shows. I won't have time to be their CEO.

But the fact remains I need to make some money. You know, some dough, some cheddar, some cabbage, bread, and lettuce. Hmm, whoever came up with all the different names for cash must've been hungry for a grilled-cheese sandwich and a side salad.

Looks like my dad is right. As a kid, it's hard to make some scratch . . . grrrrr. Sorry, my dog is at the patio door wanting to come inside.

All week I try to think of ways to earn money. Finally, I decide to invite Billy to come over. We're more creative together, and not just when we build cool stuff like our slingshot bike.

After a couple of hours of hanging out, I come up with a money-making plan. We're going to start our own food delivery service! For the record, I came up with this brilliant idea on my own based off something random my dad said, something like "Why don't you start your own food delivery service?"

Dad was trying to get me and Billy to stop playing video games, so when Billy first came over, I told him I couldn't play video games.

"I'm still trying to come up with ways to make money," I told him.

"Have you thought of becoming a CEO?" he said.

"I already tried," I said. "It's impossible."

I guess we didn't have any good ideas because that's when we started playing my best Atari game. It's this high-graphic game where Billy and I are thin white sticks and we have to hit a tiny white dot back and forth. I can't remember the actual name of the game. We call it the "lame game."

Anyway, Dad felt that two hours of that game was enough. When we went into the kitchen to make a sandwich, he suggested getting away from video games by starting a food delivery service. That's when the new idea hit me! *We could deliver food for money.*

So Billy and I quickly created "Bob and Billy's Bicycle Delivery Service."

Billy, who doesn't have the business sense I do, suggested a title that was so much worse. He thought of "Billy and Bob's Bicycle Delivery Service." Can you believe that? He'll probably never be a CEO. After an hour of arguing, I won the coin toss and my name stuck.

To promote our new business, Billy and I created a flyer, printed some off, and passed them out to local restaurants.

A few days later, we cut a deal with a diner.

"When people call in orders, we'll have you deliver the food on your bikes for tips," the restaurant manager says.

"Deal," we say.

With that our business is off and running. Well, it's off and pedaling . . . lots of pedaling.

I learn a lot the first day. The first thing I learn is to eat before delivering food. The smell of hot fries is very tempting. My first order is for Mr. Polvado. I have to go back three times for his fries until I'm full.

I also learn that delivering food is a lot like a video game. To win, I have to race through dangerous pitfalls and jump over huge hurdles to get the food to its destination before it cools off.

Okay, so I ride on the sidewalk and there aren't actually many pitfalls. One time, however, a rabbit jumps out in front of me! It scares me so bad that I spit out my fries.

Billy and I not only pedal a lot, we also do a lot of running, especially up and down apartment stairs. If you know the old video game called Donkey Kong, then you can picture what I'm talking about. Every time I run up a staircase, I half-expect a giant monkey to throw a barrel at me.

But the real video game connection comes after we deliver the food and people give us a little money. It's awesome. Whenever I get a tip, I hear a *ca-ching* in my head, like we're collecting coins in Super Mario Bros.

It's like we're playing the perfect live-action video game. And it makes us lots of money. I had no idea how lazy people had gotten. Almost no one in our town wants to leave their house to get food.

"Maybe in a year people will pay us to stay at their house and actually *feed* them," Billy says.

"Gross!" I reply. "The only person I'm feeding is my dog, and that's so he'll come close enough that I can wrestle with him."

Billy will never be a CEO. But he's already a CFP. That's a caring, fun person. And he has some good ideas about using this money for good. We decide to donate 50 percent of our profits (minus my french fry costs) to our local food bank. Billy and I like making money, but we decide we like helping others even better. Well, maybe not *better*. It's probably 60/30. I'm not really good at math.

My youth group is impressed. They vote me the week's winner after finding out how much money Billy and I donate to help feed people.

It's ironic. I started the business to have money if I win the new video game console. But this little business might actually help me win the console!

Uh oh. It's raining. Saturday's are usually our biggest days, but there's no way I'm going out in this rainstorm, unless—

"Dad, can you drive me to all my food deliveries?" I ask.

"I'm proud you started this business," Dad says. "But making money can often be difficult. But that builds perseverance, which is something we all need in this world."

I guess that was a *no* from him.

The diner calls and tells me lots of people are ordering food because they don't want to go out in the rain. Evidently "lazy and dry" is the new American Dream. Oh well, I put on a plastic poncho that Dad finds in the garage and jump on my bike.

The flooded streets actually add to the feeling of a live-action video game. During my first delivery, I have to jump over a huge river that's at least half an inch deep and four inches wide.

I ring the doorbell and Mrs. Woodward opens the door,

hands me a $1.50 tip, and thanks me for braving the storm to bring her family food.

"I'm just trying to level up," I say.

I guess she doesn't play video games because she doesn't laugh. But I can't get the smile off my face. I love providing a service and raising money for charity . . . and more fries for me.

If it continues raining on the weekends, I'll be able to buy lots of video games for my new console. I'm not sure how much money I've made so far. I keep all of it in my locker at school. This way my brother can't find it.

You can't be too careful with your money. When I get to school on Monday, I'm going to add what I made today and count it. I also need to start on that book for reading class. I can't forget that.

When I get home, I realize Billy and I have set a new money-making record. Who knew that looking wet and miserable meant you get better tips. And I didn't even try! It just came natural. Mrs. Faircloth even tipped me $10 because of all my "shivering and whimpering."

I give $25 to my dad for the food bank, and I'll add $25 to the huge stash in my locker on Monday.

Maybe I should open a bank account. I've heard that's what CEOs do. Naw, that's a silly idea.

Chapter 7

The Terrible Threesome stole the money out of my locker! I can't prove it right now but I know it has to be them.

When I got to school, my locker door was open. But I didn't suspect anything at first. How could anyone know I'm storing money in there? And I didn't think anyone could find it in my secret hiding place. I keep all my money in a dirty sock in the back of my locker. The sock smells like Mr. Gribble's office. But when I pulled out the sock to add the new money, it feels empty. The money is all gone! The whole space smells like betrayal.

Now you're probably thinking a dirty sock in a school locker is a terrible place to hide money. It's not. First of all, no one wants to touch a dirty sock. Second of all, I added some extra precautions. I wrote on the sock: "Bonus Math Questions for Fun Inside." Then I put the sock in the back of my locker. For added protection, I stacked one of the Christmas CDs of me singing on top of the sock. Past experience has taught me that no one wants to touch those.

The Christmas CD was one of my great ideas from last year. I recorded myself singing Christmas songs and then ordered one hundred CDs from a website that said it could make me a famous singer. I thought I could sell them, to have some money for Christmas gifts . . . and then also get famous. I still have a few available by the way, like ninety-nine. If I sell just seventy more, I'll make back the money it cost me to make the CDs.

But that's not the point. The point is the Terrible Threesome just got more Terriblesome. They took my sock money *and* the CD.

I decide to confront Luke first. He's the smallest of the three. I'm smart like that.

Walking up to him in the hall, I say, "I want my sock money back!"

Luke says he has no idea what I'm talking about. He then walks away singing "Silent Night." Wait, that's the first song on my Christmas CD!

Suddenly, I know exactly what to do. I speed walk to the principal's office and report to her that my sock, money, and CD are missing. Instead of helping, Mrs. Durham gives me a speech on why I shouldn't keep valuables in my locker.

"I can't do anything without more evidence," she says.

"He was singing 'Silent Night,'" I argue.

"Maybe Luke is just in the Christmas spirit," she says.

"In October?" I exclaim.

"It is a little suspicious," Mrs. Durham agrees. "I will notify all the teachers to keep a lookout for a dirty sock."

This is turning out to be the worst day ever. Every time I run into the Terrible Threesome, they're singing a song from my Christmas CD. I can't figure out how, but I know their singing is an off-key clue that I can use to solve this case.

Then lunch happens.

I'm sitting by myself, eating a sandwich, and trying to decide what to do next. Suddenly, a huge shadow moves across my table. At first, I think it's an eclipse. But I'm inside the school.

I look up and see Donny hovering over my table. I quickly start talking. I explain what really happened with the tomato. I tell him the entire truth, even my plan to use him to get even with Mark. I'm a little scared about telling him that part. But the truth is supposed to set you free, right?

Once I explain everything, Donny stands silently for a second. I can tell he's thinking. That's not something Donny does a lot, so I give him some time. He then starts laughing.

I love to hear any kind of laughter, but hearing Donny right now is one of my all-time favorite sounds. It means he's probably not mad at me.

"If you think that's funny," I say, "here's one of my favorite jokes. How does the moon cut its hair? Eclipse it!"

Donny's laughter stops. He probably doesn't get the joke. Maybe it was too much thinking for him in one day.

Anyway, Donny walks over to Mark's table. This is when my day got better and Mark's got worse. Much worse.

Seeing Donny storming his way, Mark tries to get up from his table. But he moves too fast and trips. Falling back in his chair, Mark's legs shoot into the air. That's when I see it! Mark's wearing my sock.

"Hang on!" I shout. "What sock do you have on?"

Mark tries to pull his pantleg over his sock . . . well, my sock. But it's too late.

Mr. Garner has come over to see what's causing all the noise.

"Are you okay?" he asks Mark.

"He is now," I say. "But he won't be after I tell you what he did."

I quickly tell Mr. Garner how my money was stolen

from my locker and that Mark is clearly wearing my money sock. It takes a bit to bring Mr. Garner up to speed on the details, but there's really no denying the evidence.

We all walk to the principal's office. I take my normal chair, while the others stand against the wall. Mrs. Durham grills the Terrible Threesome with questions until they finally confess.

"Go get the money and return it to Bob," she orders.

Jordan leaves the room with Mr. Garner. A few minutes later they return and Jordan hands me my money and my CD.

"Thank you, Mrs. Durham," I say. "And to show you my appreciation, I want to give you this CD."

"I'm good," she says.

I guess she's not a fan of Christmas music. I also tell Mark he can keep the sock.

"I won't be hiding valuables in my locker anymore," I explain. "Plus, I don't want something that's been on your stinky foot."

Mrs. Durham gives each of the Terrible Threesome a week of detention. That makes Donny smile. At least, I think that's what makes him smile. Donny hasn't said anything this whole time. It's funny. I thought Donny would be a big problem for me in middle school, but he's actually helped me. It just goes to show that you can't judge a book by its cover, even if it's a big cover like Donny.

"Does anyone have anything else to say?" Mrs. Durham asks.

Suddenly, Donny bursts out laughing.

"What's so funny?" Mrs. Durham says.

"Eclipse it," Donny says. "That's how the moon cuts its hair. Eclipse it. I get it."

Donny is full of surprises. I thought he was done thinking for the day.

I walk out of the principal's office thanking God for Donny and for a great day.

It just goes to show, never give up on a day. Sure, today was full of risks. I took a risk confronting Luke. I took a risk telling Donny what my plans had been, even though they involved him getting hit with a tomato. But these risks helped me uncover the truth and get my money back. Plus, Donny and I are on good terms again.

I can't wait to share this wild story at church. Nothing can ruin my mood . . . until I walk into reading class.

Mrs. Wordsmith asks each student to give an update on the book we're supposed to be reading.

This reading class is about to become an improv class, because I'm going to have to make something up pretty quick. I peek in the book to get some material.

I'm going to have to start reading this book soon or I'm going to be in trouble in this class.

Chapter 8

I love October, and not just because I got my money back. Every year at this time we carve pumpkins. Dad always buys me two in case I drop one. Like that's going to happen!

"I wish you had more confidence in me," I tell Dad when he brings out the spare pumpkin.

I think my words would have been more convincing if I hadn't spoken them at the same time I was cleaning up the first pumpkin.

Dropping it wasn't my fault. Our dog came out of nowhere and started barking at me. I guess he still doesn't like being my wrestling partner.

Wrestling is going great by the way. Yes, I did discover that school wrestling is not like the wrestling on TV. I'm not allowed to wear my mask or cape. And there's no intro music. The matches are over pretty quickly, too. Well, at least mine are.

Last weekend, we had a meet where I did a lot better than when I first started. I didn't get pinned until almost half a minute into the first period. I could tell my opponent was frustrated at how good I was at blocking all her moves.

Anyway, I've recently taken the lead in the youth group's taking-risks-for-God contest. And I'm about to take another huge risk. Our school is having a talent show, and I signed up to do comedy.

Mrs. Brown, our band teacher, was very excited when I told her. She had often encouraged me to explore some of my other talents. "Maybe you could mime," she once told me. "That would be . . . quieter."

When I told her about my comedy routine, I could tell she was afraid I'd be so good that the other kids in the competition wouldn't stand a chance.

"Don't worry," I said with a wink. "I'll keep things fair by not using my 'A' material."

"I didn't know you had an 'A' in anything," she said.

Some people just aren't funny. But that's not important now. The important thing is the talent show is starting in a few minutes and I'm super nervous.

I tell jokes all the time. Being funny is my thing. However, it's way different standing on a stage and trying to make people laugh. We did a run-through earlier today that made me even more nervous. All the elementary school kids came to our auditorium to watch practice. They didn't get my jokes at all.

"I'm so skinny I can use ChapStick as deodorant," I said for my opening joke.

The elementary kids sat there silently. Well, mostly. "I use ChapStick," one little kid called out.

Then it hit me. You have to know your audience. These kids were years away from needing deodorant. I had to tell jokes they could relate to. I quickly switched to knock-knock jokes.

"Knock, knock," I said.

"Who's there?" three kids answered.

"Pecan."

"Pecan who?"

"Pecan someone your own size."

Half the kids laughed. That gave me more confidence, so again I said, "Knock, knock."

"Who's there?" nearly every kid replied.

"Iron."

"Iron who?"

"Iron money delivering food. How about you?"

Crickets. I guess all these kids came from rich families

and didn't have to earn their own money. I ended my set with my famous "moon/eclipse" joke.

Again, total silence. Well, actually the ChapStick kid shouted that he liked the moon. I guess he thought he was part of the show now.

Now it's time for the real show. I'm sitting backstage, and we're about to start. Thank goodness I'm not going first. The order of the show goes:

1. Sarah singing a song.

2. Mason doing a trick where people shout out math questions and he quickly calculates the answer in his head.

3. Donny waking up the audience by breaking two boards with his hand.

4. Me. The headline comedy act.

Then there's some other acts, but that's not important right now.

Mrs. Brown starts the show by thanking everyone for coming. She tells all the students and parents how hard we've worked on our acts. Then she invites Sarah onto the stage.

Wow. Sarah can sing! She goes out and sings so well it sounds like she's lip-syncing. The applause lasts nearly as long as her song.

The crowd also loves Mason's math tricks. Adults shout out all kinds of math questions and then quickly check his answers on their phones to see if he's right. It's funny that a roomful of parents in a school building need to cheat to find the right answer. It sort of makes me feel better about my last math test.

Donny is on next to break boards. Two stage helpers set up two small tables with the boards balanced between them.

Crack! He snaps the boards with one quick chop and the crowd goes crazy! This hypes Donny up so much that he chops at the tables and breaks them, too. He walks off to a standing ovation.

This is bad. I had my jokes written on a piece of paper taped to one of those tables. Now they're shattered, just like my confidence.

Before I can say anything, Mrs. Brown walks onto the stage. The stage helpers are quickly cleaning up the table pieces. They sweep them to the side as Mrs. Brown introduces me.

I've already showered today but my body chooses this moment to give itself a shower. I break into a cold sweat all over. I stand frozen backstage. Strangely, I feel more frozen than the time I put snow all over myself to make Billy think I was a snowman who'd come to life. That's another story for another time, but let's say I was really frozen then.

"Hey AB, it's your turn," Sarah says. "Go make them laugh."

"Uh, don't you want to do another song?" I ask.

"You got this," she says.

That's when I remember the taking risks challenge. God gives each person individual talents. He wants us to use those talents, to share them with others. And it's our choice. I choose to take the risk and share my talents. Unfortunately, my body hasn't made the same decision. I still can't move.

Have you ever had an out-of-body experience where you feel like you're floating above yourself? That's what happens next. Well, not really. I feel like I'm floating, but only because Donny picks me up and carries me to the center of the stage.

He sets me down, and I stand in front of the microphone. The crowd stops clapping. The entire auditorium is deathly silent. It's even worse than when I performed for the elementary students.

I look down at the front row and see the Terrible Threesome glaring at me. Jordan mouths the words, "You're not funny." Mark and Luke make choking faces at me. Then something changes.

I grab the microphone and get my first laugh.

Chapter 9

That first laugh doesn't come exactly how I plan. As I try to remember my first joke, I grab the microphone. Somehow it sticks in its holder. Wrestling has made me stronger. So I use more force, rip the mike off the stand . . . and into my head. Thwack!

I turn red, but the crowd laughs.

Holding my head, I do some quick improvising, "My dad always says to use my head, but I don't think that's what he meant."

More laughter.

"I got hit in the head yesterday with a can of soda," I continue. "Thankfully, it was a soft drink."

This time laughter mixes with applause. All of a sudden my jokes come back to me. There must be a lot of smelly adults in the audience, because my ChapStick joke gets a huge laugh. I do a few more. Then I look down at the Terrible Threesome and smile.

This makes Mark super mad. He leans forward, grabs the microphone cord, and gives it a yank. The microphone stumbles from my hand. Mark is so good at being sneaky that nobody notices what he did. The crowd just thinks I've dropped the mic.

I smile again. The Terrible Threesome can't bother me today. I really feel like God is with me, and I'm using my talents to encourage others. I scramble to pick up the microphone and tell my last joke.

"That reminds me," I say. "Two pickles fell out of a jar and one said to the other one, 'Oh, just dill with it.' Good night everybody!" Then I drop the mic for real.

Walking offstage feels great.

My youth pastor was right. Doing something risky can be scary, but sometimes you end up doing something amazing. After the show we all stand around giving autographs. Well, I assume people want my autograph, so I keep randomly signing women's purses or men's jackets until they stop coming near me.

I'm feeling on top of the world . . . until Mrs. Brown tells me the microphone broke when I dropped it. Looks like my food delivery tips this week will go to pay for a new microphone.

That talent show was scary, but now I'm facing something scarier. My family has decided to eat healthier for the rest of the year. Actually, let me rephrase that: My *dad* decided we should all be healthier. Fortunately, he decided that after all the Harvest parties were over and my brother and I had eaten all of our candy.

I sort of blame my brother for Dad's decision. If my brother knew how to control his anger, he wouldn't have chased me up the stairs after I popped him with a rubber band from across the room. It was an accident, of course, but what a great shot! I was wrestling my dog and trying to stretch a rubber band to hold his paws together. He kicked me in the stomach, the rubber band got away, and it hit Brian in the forehead.

If Brian had been wearing a hat, it would've hit brim, not head. Unfortunately, he wasn't wearing a hat. I feel that this, too, was not my fault.

I took off running upstairs and my brother followed. Dad thought something bad was up, so he ran after my brother. Then something really was up—his heart rate.

My brother cornered me in the attic. I told him it was an accident and that he should start wearing more hats. Before my brother could reply, a loud thunderstorm hit. Okay, we just thought it was thunder. Turns out Dad was just trying to get up the last few stairs. We stopped fighting and ran over to him.

That's when he told us we're all going to start eating healthier and getting in better shape. At least I think that's what he said. He was breathing so hard that I couldn't really understand his words.

Anyway, if my brother hadn't chased me, Dad wouldn't have chased after us and realized how out of shape he was. Then we could've kept eating junk food for the rest of the year.

As you can see, it's all Brian's fault.

Mom is totally on board with healthy eating. I can tell by looking at my dinner plate. It appears she took it out of our lawn mower bag. I can see grasses, leaves, onions, berries, and something that appears to be a dried finger.

"That's a date," Mom says.

"I think I'm too young to date," I reply.

Mom doesn't laugh. "Just eat it," she says. "It has a lot of fiber and copper."

Copper? If I wanted copper, I'd suck on a penny.

Not only are we eating healthy, we're also exercising as a family.

Every night after dinner—which is over pretty fast now that we don't have food we enjoy—we go on a walk. My dad was so out of shape that on the first night we didn't make it to the end of the driveway before he said, "That's enough walking for tonight."

Now we all enjoy the walks. My favorite part is dumping the lawn mower food from dinner back into its natural habitat. During dinner, I stuff the grasses and leaves I don't want into my pockets. Then I return it to the wild on our walks when Mom isn't looking.

Don't tell my Mom this, but I'm actually feeling better lately. Some of the vegetables she makes are pretty good. And the walks are a lot of fun. We're talking more as a family and laughing together.

With all of this exercise and healthy eating, I have more energy, I'm more alert at school, and I'm even sleeping better.

Sleeping is great, but it does come with its own set of problems. You've probably heard of the Tooth Fairy. Well, since I've been sleeping more, I've gotten to know the Eye Crust Fairy.

You usually never hear anything about the Eye Crust Fairy. Unlike the Tooth Fairy, who only visits when I eat too much candy or fall off my bike, the Eye Crust Fairy visits me nearly every night.

Most mornings I wake up with what feels like a huge

sand castle in my eyes. The gunk is so thick that sometimes I can't pry my eyes open. That's when Mom gets a warm rag to remove the gunk—along with my eyelashes and sometimes my eyebrows.

She makes me green food, gets gunk out of my eyes, and does all sorts of other work around the house that helps our family.

I'll give you an example. Earlier this week she even waited at the bus stop with me. After removing the eye crust (she let me keep my eyelashes this time), she gave me a big kiss as the school bus pulled up. She does this to make sure I have my daily dose of embarrassment.

"Have a great day at school, Honey," she said as I got on the bus. "I'm going to start on your dirty laundry today. If I'm not back in a week, send someone in after me!"

Mom likes to make jokes. They aren't always funny, but I know she's just trying to make my life better.

Chapter 10

Thanksgiving is here! I'm not as excited as I normally am because of our family's healthy eating plan.

Instead of our traditional turkey, Mom says we're having something called *tofurky*. That's tofu shaped like a turkey.

If you haven't had tofurky, it's a lot like turkey in the same way that basketball is a lot like clipping your toenails. Maybe that's not the best example. Toenails probably taste better than tofu.

But I'm still excited about Thanksgiving this year. Our youth group is performing a Thanksgiving play! I've been in a lot of plays over the years. For the past three years, I've had one of the lead roles in our church's Christmas play. My character is usually named "guy who opens and closes the curtain." The crowd loves it. I can tell because they start applauding the second I pull on the strings. Then when the play ends and I close the curtain, I usually get a standing ovation. The crowd cheers so much that I often have to open the curtain again.

Last year my performance wasn't *quite* as flawless. I usually like to sit on a tall stool on the side of the stage. Then I lean on the curtain ropes so I can hang farther onto the stage and the crowd can see me. You've got to give the fans what they want. Last year I somehow fell asleep twenty minutes into the play. (According to my Dad, I wasn't eating as many leaves and dates at the time, so I didn't have much energy.) Anyhow, I tumbled off my stool. And because I was caught up in the ropes, my fall ended up closing the curtain.

This event changed the play a little. Basically, baby Jesus only received gold and frankincense. Plus, Donny, who oddly enough was playing a wise man, got mad because he'd stayed up all night learning how to say the word "myrrh" and never got his chance to say it.

I haven't always had such an important role. At my first audition in elementary school, the music teacher said she'd assign an instrument or a singing part to everyone based on our individual talents. Right in the middle of my singing audition, the music teacher stopped me and said she had the perfect role for me. She went to the back of the room, opened a closet door, and dug around for ten minutes until she found a box.

"Nobody's used these for years," she said, handing me the box. "But you possess a . . . *unique* set of talents."

I opened the box and found two copper discs that looked like band cymbals that had been hit by a shrink ray.

"They're finger cymbals," my teacher said.

You probably don't realize how talented you have to be to play the finger cymbals. Getting the right chime takes a certain dexterity. It's usually not a lead role in a band or play, but I'm always happy to play my part.

Amazingly, I got cast as the finger cymbal player in every elementary school play after that. Many times there wasn't even music in the play, so my teacher had me play the finger cymbals backstage or out in the parking lot.

Two years ago I broke into an impromptu finger-cymbal solo during a back-to-school performance. I jumped off the back row of the choir stands and onto one of the big speaker boxes. The artist in me took over, and I played my finger cymbals as loud and fast as I could.

When I was done, the crowd was so amazed that they were actually silent. They obviously hadn't expected such an intense showing of talent.

God works in mysterious ways, because my youth pastor was in the crowd that night. And when it came time to cast the roles for the Christmas play at church, he told me I'd have the most important part: opening and closing the curtain.

"Without you, the people would never see the show," he said.

At that moment, I knew the curtain role was the most important one because it's the same role that Jesus played when He came to earth. After Jesus died on the cross to bring forgiveness for sins, people didn't have to be separated from God anymore. He opened the curtain for everybody. Without Jesus, nobody would get to see God, and everyone would miss the eternal show in heaven.

Now that I think about it, I did also get an important role in the fourth-grade musical. I remember running through the screen door at home to tell my parents that I was "singer number eleven." Obviously a lead role. And once my parents fixed the screen door with duct tape, they shared in my excitement.

"I'm so proud of you!" Mom said. "I guess you can stop singing around here now."

"Actually, I need to keep practicing," I told her. "The show isn't until next month."

"You aren't going to sing everything you say from now on, are you?" my brother asked, joining the excitement.

"I sure AMMMMMM!!!!" I sang.

Then my dog started howling. He's a big fan of musicals too.

Anyway, the point is I've been in a lot of plays. However, this Thanksgiving play is probably going to be the best one so far. In fact, I wouldn't be surprised if some major movie studio picks it up. Then I'll have to fly somewhere to make the movie. At least I hope that happens.

I just remembered something. I still haven't started on the book for reading class that's due next month. I really need to get started on that.

Chapter 11

The Thanksgiving play is awesome. It turns out that I have an even better role this year, one where I'm actually *on stage*. I'm playing the lead role of Pilgrim Number Eight. The play starts with the Pilgrims landing at Plymouth Rock. Our church doesn't have a big budget for props, so we're using the same stone from the Easter play. Fortunately, someone from church recently purchased a refrigerator, so we do have a realistic cardboard boat.

Memorizing my lines for the play was super easy because I don't have any. Our youth pastor obviously knows I'm a master of ad-lib and body language.

As soon as we run our boat into Plymouth Rock, we

all climb out of the refrigerator box and stretch our backs like we've been on a long trip. Then I try my first ad-lib.

"I'm starving!" I say. "Let's find a drive-thru and get a burger."

Everyone laughs, except the youth pastor. He must have a toothache, because his teeth are tightly clenched. Billy, who always seems to know what I'm thinking, pretends to sail the Mayflower to a drive-thru window and asks, "Can I get fries with that?"

The other kids just stare at us and continue saying their scripted lines. Where's their sense of adventure? This is the New World!

In the next scene, we build houses. That's when I remember the Pilgrims came from England.

"My house is going to have a guest room," I say in my best English accent, "in case any of our friends from jolly ol' England drop by."

For the rest of the play, I only speak with an English accent that my dad later describes as sounding "Australian."

The second act begins during winter. We let the audience know it's winter by using a clever dramatic technique: Randy comes onstage and says, "Well, it's winter now." We all shiver to let the audience know that Randy is correct. Then the Native Americans show up.

"Welcome to the neighborhood!" I shout.

That gets another big laugh.

The Native Americans show us how to hunt. We apparently show them how to put buckles on their shoes and hats. For the hunting scene, we "shoot" several invisible animals with our bows and muskets.

"Pow-pow," I say, adding realistic sound effects for my musket.

Trent picks up on how my sound effects are making things better and adds some "twangs" as he shoots his bow.

I keep looking into the audience for movie scouts. All I see are familiar smiling faces. Well, everyone is smiling except our youth leader. He's still grinding his teeth . . . and holding his face with both hands.

Finally, we make it to the big Thanksgiving feast. I'm feeling pretty hungry.

"Pilgrim Number Nine, pleese pass ye thee ketchup," I say to Billy.

Billy pretends to hand me a bottle.

That's when Jeremy, who thinks he has the lead role as William Bradford, gets mad.

"Quit ruining the play!" he yells, throwing a turkey leg at me. "You guys aren't following the script!"

"Oy, mate! Whatchu on about?" I reply in a perfect English accent.

Out of nowhere, somebody throws my turkey leg at Jeremy. There's no proof who did it; probably some Australian guy.

After that, the first Thanksgiving turns into the first American food fight. This is just the kind of action Hollywood is looking for. It's going great until our youth pastor runs onstage and ends the play early.

I think he has to get to the dentist. Donny has the last ad-lib of the night by shouting, "Myrrh." It's the wrong play, but he nails his line.

Anyway, the play's a huge hit.

"How do you think the play went?" I ask my youth pastor as we clean up.

"You added a lot," he compliments me. "But I wonder if the crowd wants you back in your most-requested role of 'guy who opens and closes the curtain' for our next play."

You can't argue with the fans. It's also nice to have job security.

A few days later I sit down for Thanksgiving dinner with my family. My grandparents, aunt, uncle, and cousins are here. They obviously didn't get the word about us eating healthy.

All the greens and vegetables are on the table as Mom brings in the tofurky.

My grandfather takes one look at the plant-based tofu roll and asks, "Does this turkey have the flu?"

"We're going to eat like the original Pilgrims without any sugar or processed wheat," Mom says.

My grandfather doesn't process that well. He doesn't hide his love of turkey well either. We all hold hands, and he offers to say the prayer:

"Dear heavenly Father. Thank You for showing us grace. We will need some grace as we try to eat this tofu thing instead of the nice juicy turkey that You made so we could eat it. Give us patience as our taste buds protest this meal. Thank You for family, even those family members who made bad decisions on what to prepare for today. We love You, Lord. There's so much to be thankful for here on this planet, even though none of those things can be found here on this table. We're thankful for Your Son Jesus, for Your love, and for the grocery store that's four miles from here and open on holidays. May it still have some pies for sale. In Jesus' name we pray, Amen."

Dad bursts out laughing. That makes us all laugh. Then Mom makes this the most memorable Thanksgiving ever by walking over to the oven and pulling out a huge Thanksgiving turkey!

"I figure we can expand our diet a little today," she says. "And there are a couple of pies cooling in the garage."

My brother, Dad, and I cheer. Grandpa has tears in his eyes.

"You married well, son," he says to Dad. Then he takes my mom's hand. "God bless you."

Mom explains that the tofurky is just for her and Dad. "We're going to stick to *our* diets," she says looking at him. Dad's cheer disappears.

Still, we all feast, laugh, and talk about things we're thankful for. After the meal, we all help clean up.

"Let me take some turkey scraps to the dog, so he can enjoy Thanksgiving too," Dad offers.

"What a nice thing to do," Mom says. "He's had a difficult wrestling season."

It's the perfect ending to our celebration. Dad even looks happy when he comes back.

Mom isn't. There's a little turkey on Dad's chin.

Chapter 12

I can tell it's almost Christmas because we're taking part in a cherished Christmas tradition. Mom and I have spent the last two hours driving around the mall looking for a parking space as she shouts, "Ho! Ho! Ho!"

Actually, now she's yelling, "Go! Go! Go!"

Mom likes to find people walking out of the stores. Then she drives behind them until they get to their car, so she can take their parking space. She drives close enough so they know we want their space—meaning our bumper may occasionally touch the back of someone's leg.

I try to help Mom stay in a good mood by singing the

"Twelve Days of Christmas." The only words I know are "a partridge in a pear tree" and "FIVE GOLDEN RINGS!" (which must always be sung in capital letters). So I have to make up the rest of the lyrics.

"One driver driving, two tempers rising, three moms a yelling, four people staring, FIVE GOLDEN RINGS!"

Sometimes my singing actually moves Mom to the point of tears . . . like right now. It's a loving Christmas tradition.

Oh wow! Mom accidentally hits the steering wheel and blares the horn. It scares the guy attached to our front bumper so much that he drops his gifts and offers us some Christmas cheer. I can't make out what he's saying, but it sure looks like he's full of Christmas spirit!

"Seven horns a honking, six shoppers shouting, FIVE GOLDEN RINGS!" I continue with my song.

Even with parking problems, my family loves Christmas, especially Dad. He gets so excited that he's like a kid at . . . uh, well, Christmas. Every year Dad buys a tree that can be seen from outer space—or even farther away, like Russia.

Last year we had two Christmas trees: the burnable one and the new one. Actually, the new one may have been flammable too. I never found out because I wasn't allowed to put birthday candles for Jesus on the tree anymore. This added to a long list of Christmas items that my parents don't allow me to put on the tree, such as the garden hose, real snow, my brother, my report card cut into tiny snow-flakes, and the cat.

One thing I can put on the tree is the star. A star led the Magi to the baby Jesus. Now Jesus is the light that leads us to God. That's what Christmas is really about. I think about that every time I put up the star.

My dad may love buying huge trees, but we don't have a big house. Each year we bring home a tree, drag it to the back patio, and start emergency surgery.

Normally, we start by cutting off the top of the tree in small segments until it fits through the door. This usually results in four or five mini-trees. My brother and I set them all around the house to add Christmas cheer. We originally thought more trees equaled more gifts, but we were wrong about that.

Yesterday, Dad bought the biggest tree ever. Mom asked if we were going to put the house in the tree this time. Dad laughed, until we wrestled the tree up to the back door. The tree was way too wide to fit through. That's when I had a great idea.

"We could tie a rope to the tree, run it through the house, out the front door, and tie the other end to the bumper of your car," I said. "Then you could pull the tree through the door with the car."

Dad paused to think it over. Then he said something that I'd never heard before. "Bob, that's a great idea."

Mom rolled her eyes and suggested that we buy a smaller tree. Ha! Another tree. Moms are funny.

Anyway, I tied the rope to the tree. Dad positioned the car outside our front door. And he tied the rope to the bumper.

With everything in place, we took our positions. Dad told me to signal him when the tree was inside the house. Looking back, we should've decided on a signal. Dad nudged the car forward, and the tree squeezed through the door.

I jumped up and down, waving my arms and shouting, "That was fast!"

Dad thought my arm waving and shouting was the signal to go faster. He gunned the engine. For a second

it looked like the tree was chasing our dog as it zoomed through our living room. I started to laugh, until I saw the tree race past the TV, zip past the couch, and head for a bookshelf full of antiques.

Just as I was wondering what to do with the lump of coal that I was definitely getting for Christmas, the tree stopped. I looked up and saw Mom by the front door. She had the tree trimmers in one hand and a cut rope in the other.

"That was a close one." I smiled.

"You say that a lot," Mom said.

Moms are funny. Sometimes they're also superheroes. Like now, she just found a parking spot! We head inside the mall to buy gifts. Well, she's buying gifts. I'm just here for moral support. Then we're going home to decorate the tree.

Decorating the tree is a process in our house. It starts with Dad reading the list of things I can't put on it. Then the decorating starts. Afterwards, our family sits down to hear Dad read the story of how Jesus was born. It's one of my favorite parts of Christmas. Jesus' birth reminds me what's really important about this holiday.

"It's great that Jesus got myrrh and frankincense," I say. "But I think a glow-in-the-dark Frankenstein would be super cool!"

"I think you missed the point of the story," Dad says. "And you definitely forgot about the time we bought you a glow-in-the-dark clown mask."

I didn't forget. It's the reason my aunt will no longer spend the night at our house.

We finish the evening by telling each other cool things Christ has done in our lives this past year. It's another tradition in my family—just like looking for a parking space. But this one doesn't include as much yelling.

I love Christmas! It's about love, hope, the birth of our Savior, and FIVE GOLDEN RINGS! Speaking of gifts, tomorrow I'm getting my presents ready.

Chapter 13

Every Christmas I try to get my parents gifts that show how much I appreciate them. The problem is that stores don't realize kids don't have much money. I do have some leftover money from the delivery service Billy and I started. That job is over for three reasons.

First, Billy decided it was too cold out. He's right. In Texas, it can get down into the 70s during the winter.

Second, I was gaining too much weight eating everyone's fries.

Third, the restaurant owner told us he didn't need us anymore.

Mainly, it was the first two reasons.

Fortunately, I'm great at making gifts that don't cost much money. Over the years, I've come up with a lot of homemade gift tips and ideas:

No. 1: Go Funny. A cheap gift can be great if it's memorable. Once I gave my dad a can of beans with a card that said, "Have a rootin', tootin' good Christmas!" Two years ago, my grandfather got a bucket of nails with a sign that read "Manly Toothpicks." One Christmas when my mom was sick I wrapped up a sneeze controller. It was a clothespin. And last year I got my brother some batteries with a sign that said, "Gift not included." If they laugh, I know the gift is a hit.

No. 2: Potpourri. Mom loves things that smell good. That's why she almost never comes into my room. I once made some potpourri for her. I walked in the woods and gathered good-smelling leaves and twigs. Then I put them in a blender, added cinnamon, nutmeg, dried apples, and orange peels, and blended on high for one minute. She loves the homemade potpourri . . . and the new blender Dad had to buy for her.

No. 3: Snowman. I learned at school that recycling is important. My favorite recycled gift for Dad uses an upside-down white Styrofoam cup and an old golf ball. I just glue the golf ball on top and use a marker to draw a face. Then I stick three buttons on the cup, take two twigs out of the potpourri for arms, and it's done.

No. 4: Calendar. All I do for this one is gather twelve sheets of paper and my new colored pencils. I draw a picture on one side and the month's dates on the other. As a special touch, I add holidays in the appropriate squares. (Tip: Parents won't believe it's your birthday every month, no matter how many times you write it down. Just trust me.)

No. 5: Jar of Nothing. Whenever I ask my parents what they want for Christmas, they always say, "Oh, nothing." One year I showed them how well I could listen. I gave them an empty jar labeled, "Everything you wanted for Christmas."

No. 6: Coupons. These are easy to make, but come with risks. Now I always write, "Photocopies Not Accepted" in tiny letters on every coupon. My dad still has about eight hundred "Will Clean Room" coupons that he printed off three years ago. Also, I don't leave room for any other words to be added to the coupon. I'm quite certain I never wrote, "Will also clean toilets forever" on a coupon I gave to my mom. That was gross, but not as gross as what happened when I gave my dad a "Free Foot Rub" coupon. Worst five minutes of my life.

Anyway, I'm nearly done with this year's Christmas presents.

My dad is getting a new stocking to hang on the mantle at Christmas. The idea came to me when I busted a hole

in one of my favorite pair of socks. I hated to throw them away. Then I remembered how Dad's stocking ended up in the fire last year. A new stocking is the perfect gift!

My brother's gift is some cool new running shoes. Mom says they're not a good gift because they're my size. Plus, I'm wearing them right now. I don't want my brother to grow out of them too fast, so I bought them big. And I'm wearing them to break them in.

Mom's surprise gift is a box to hold her jewelry. I just have to cover the word "Nike" so she doesn't know where the box came from. I'm also making her a cake decorator. A cake decorator is basically a tube full of icing. You squeeze the tube, and the icing shoots out of a hole onto the cake. This is the perfect gift for Mom. Plus, it's the perfect way to use that other holey sock I have.

I bought Billy a box of Band-Aids. He thinks his dad is getting him a pocketknife. I'm not sure this is true. Last year Billy thought he heard his dad say the family was getting a flamethrower. We were so disappointed when we went to the garage and saw a brand-new, battery-powered leaf blower. No matter what Billy gets from his dad, I think Band-Aids are a perfect gift for him.

Christmas is a time to show people how much you care. It's about spending time with family and friends and remembering God's gift to us, His Son, our Savior.

Of course, presents are a part of it, and I've got to get these wrapped before anyone discovers the great gifts I got them. Christmas is only a few days away.

Chapter 14

I'm trying to have Christmas spirit, but it's hard. Jenny is in the lead in the youth group contest. The other kids voted for her the last three weeks. I thought for sure I'd get some votes for standing in an empty parking space and fighting off other cars so my dad could park and buy his gifts for me. That's being a real servant.

All Jenny did is organize a canned food drive in her neighborhood. She baked a plate of Christmas cookies for all her neighbors and delivered them with a note that asked for them to leave donations on their porch. She picked up the cans and ended up with a whole trunk full of food.

I guess being able to eat is one way to make people

happy. I try another. I go caroling with a group of people. Everybody loves my singing, especially when their dogs join in with me. As I mentioned before, I've never been great at remembering the words to songs, so sometimes I allow my immense ad-libbing talents to take over.

For one song I sing, "Over the liver and through the foods, to Cadbury eggs we go!"

Some of the carolers get really upset about this. Are they jealous of my talent? But a girl named Carol joins in with my creativity. She sings, "I know there's no way . . . I'll eat some pâté! Give me white and toasted Marsh-MALLOW!"

It's awesome! Plus, I've never been good with names. Caroling with Carol makes it easy to remember hers. Maybe next year I'll pick friends based on what we do together. It'll be like, "Hey Wilson, would you like to play volleyball? Nice to meet you Mario, do you have a brother we can play video games with?"

Caroling isn't the only way I serve people at Christmas. The week before Christmas, Dad lets me hang our outside Christmas lights. He likes to give me jobs where I learn something. And I learn a lot!

1. Our ladder doesn't stay upright on windy days.

2. Our Christmas lights are strong enough to swing on.

3. My brother has a hearing problem.

No matter how loud I shout for him to put the ladder back up, Brian can't hear me. He is laughing really loudly

at something. I keep trying to see what it is as I swing by on the string of Christmas lights, but I never spot anything funny enough to LOL about.

However, the best way I serve over Christmas break is helping my youth group take a trailer full of gifts to a women's shelter. The shelter helps give Moms and their kids a safe place to stay. But living there means they don't have much of anything for Christmas. The church encouraged families to bring in presents all month. Dad owns a truck, so he volunteered to pull the trailer to the shelter.

This is the big morning. Dad and I drive to the church parking lot. The rest of the youth group is meeting us at the shelter. I help Dad back up the truck and hook up the trailer.

Five minutes into our trip, I look out my window.

"Hey, there's a trailer passing us that looks just like ours," I say.

"That's strange," Dad points out. "There's no truck pulling it."

I look behind our truck and notice our trailer is missing. Dad sees the same thing.

"That's our trailer!" Dad says calmly.

"I'm sorry!" I calmly shout back. "I must not have fas-
tened the hitch tight enough. What are we going to do?"

"I've got an idea," Dad says. "Hold on."

Dad speeds alongside the trailer. Then he turns slightly
to nudge the trailer off the road. At first I think he's crazy,
and that he's ruining the truck's paint job.

Then I look ahead and see a sign: *Hay for Sale*. Eight
gigantic, round haystacks sit by the side of the road. My
dad guides the trailer into the first haystack. Hay flies
everywhere, but the trailer stops safely.

"That was amazing!" I shout

"Where do you think your superpowers come from?"
Dad says with a smile.

Ten minutes later we're back on the road.

"Sorry about the hitch mess-up," I say.

"No problem," Dad says. "I should've double-checked
before driving off. Now let's go make some kids happy."

"You've already made one kid happy." I grin.

It's a great moment . . . until Dad says, "You did remember to close the door of the trailer after you checked to see
if the gifts were okay, right?"

Once we gather up all the presents from the road,
we head to the women's shelter. Everyone's waiting. We

quickly unload the trailer and hand out gifts. Then we bring all the kids together to read the story of Jesus' birth. My youth pastor lets me read the story, because I've done such a great job with the presents.

I start reading, but then my ad-lib skills take over. In my defense, the story does become more modern and relatable. And I don't change it that much.

Instead of a stable, I tell everyone that Joseph and Mary have to stay at a Super 7 Motel. If you've ever stayed at one, you know it's a lot like sleeping in an animal stall. When I get to the part about the three wise men bringing gifts to baby Jesus, I make them gold, a Frankenstein action figure, and a video game called Mysteries of Myrrh.

That's when my youth pastor takes over reading. Again, some people don't appreciate my talent for winging it.

On the way home, my great-grandmother calls my dad to say she's coming for Christmas. Nana says she started our way in October, so she'll arrive in time to open gifts. I love my great-grandma, but she moves a tad slow. It's okay for me to say that. She knows she's slow-moving and jokes about it all the time.

Once she said, "I never drink milk because by the time it gets to my lips, it's cottage cheese."

With great-grandma coming, I'll have to make her a present. I wonder if I have an extra pair of socks. I'll have to remember to look in my dresser when I get home.

Chapter 15

Guess what I don't remember? I had no idea either, until I walk into my English class after Christmas break.

"Welcome back, students," Mrs. Wordsmith says. "Today, we're starting our oral book reports."

Talk about ruining all my lingering Christmas joy. I totally forgot about the book. I can't believe Billy didn't remind me.

When we first became friends, we discovered each of us excelled in certain areas. Billy is great about remembering stuff. I'm great at ad-libbing and, well, a bunch of other stuff that I can't remember right now. We're a perfect team.

At least I thought we were. I shoot a look over at Billy and mouth the words, "Why didn't you remind me?"

He whispers back something totally ridiculous. "I told you every day."

He didn't. I know for a fact he didn't mention it on Christmas or last Saturday.

Doesn't Mrs. Wordsmith know the first day back to school after Christmas break is supposed to be fun?

Actually, it starts that way. I wear the new shoes that I got my little brother for Christmas. Turns out they are way too big for him, so I agree to keep breaking them in until his feet grow.

My brother is probably having a good day in elementary school. He's wearing the hoodie he bought for me that was way too small. So both Brian and I end up with good gifts.

Anyway, it's obvious not everyone is loving the first day back. I keep hearing moaning and complaining that the break wasn't long enough. Mrs. Wordsmith must be taking out her irritation with being back in school by making us do book reports on the first day. She says we'll go in alphabetical order. This is great news! My last name is Smiley, which puts me way down on the list. There's no way I'll go before the bell rings.

"And to make it more interesting," Mrs. Wordsmith adds, "we'll go in *reverse* alphabetical order."

She may be a writing teacher, but I think Mrs. Wordsmith needs to look up the definition of "interesting." This isn't interesting. It's torture. I can tell Zander Zimmerman feels the same way by the pained look on his face. He looks the way I imagine myself looking when I'm getting pinned to the wrestling mat or eating tofu.

Okay. Four kids have gone. Trent Tuttle is next. Right before he goes up, I encourage him to take his time. No one likes a rushed speech. Actually, if my youth pastor is reading this, it's okay to rush one of his talks if the Dallas Cowboys are playing an early football game on TV.

Trent obviously isn't a very good student. He totally ignores my advice and finishes his book report in five minutes. Some kids don't take their school work seriously. It's sad really. School is our only job. We should pour ourselves into our education and do our best on every assignment.

I have a lot more to say on this subject, but it's my turn and I have no idea what I'm going to say since I didn't read the book.

I walk slowly to the front of the room. If I walk slowly enough, I won't have to go because class will be over. I glance at the clock. Fifteen minutes remain before class ends.

My plan doesn't work very well, because there are still fourteen minutes left when I make it to the front. I face the class and say, "Thank you. Thank you. Don't feel like you need to stop applauding. In fact, if you feel like you need to applaud for the next ten minutes or so, I'm not going to stop you."

The room is totally silent.

"Bob, I'm sure the entire class is interested in what you have to say about this book," Mrs. Wordsmith says.

"This book is awesome," I begin. "Just carrying it around in my backpack caused me to questions things I've never considered before, things like *Do I really need all this stuff in my backpack?* and *How much weight can I carry?* But I say to you today that a book like this one wasn't written for us to bear as a burden. It was written to put our minds in motion. Even the title and cover art makes us think."

That's when I realize I can't remember the title or what's pictured on the cover. Also, I've left the book in my backpack at my desk so I can't see it.

"I want to visually show you the cover art, but the book is back at my desk. So I'm going to go back and get it," I say, hoping that if I walk slowly enough that I can waste another five minutes.

"No, Bob," Mrs. Wordsmith says. "We all know what the book looks like. Plus, you seem to have injured your leg over the break."

"Thanks for your concern, Mrs. Wordsmith," I say. "Maybe I should go to the nurse's office to have—"

"Please continue with your report," she says.

I do what she says. "The title and the art make you think things like, *What's the book about? How many pages is it? Is it a coloring book? Is it a pop-up book?* For me, I hoped it wasn't like the pop-up book I once found at the library. I didn't realize it was a pop-up book until I opened it and this tractor popped up in my face. It was really scary, so I don't think it was fair that I got kicked out of the library for yelling at a pop-up book."

"Please stop saying 'pop-up,'" Mrs. Wordsmith says. "We don't do reports on pop-up books in a middle school reading class."

"Exactly," I say. "This book is meant for reading, and I love reading. But what is reading? It's an author painting a picture in your mind by writing words on a page for you to read. It's crazy cool how that works. And the best part is, because God made all our brains differently, we all see different things in our minds. So who am I to tell you about this book? You've read it. We've all read it! I definitely have. However, I don't want to ruin the pictures you've created in your brain by telling you what I thought about this book. I don't think that's fair to you or what the author would have wanted. So my report on this book is that it's great. It's meant to make us think and create pictures in our brains. If you haven't read it, like I have, you should. Thank you."

Everyone claps. I know I've nailed it. As I walk slowly back to my desk, the bell rings. I grab my backpack and head to the door.

"Hang on for a second, Bob," Mrs. Wordsmith says. "Can you come to my desk?"

Teachers are awesome. They always congratulate you when you do a good job.

"That was a very interesting book report," Mrs. Wordsmith says. "God has given you an amazingly creative mind. He's also given you a lot of talent using humor and confidence."

"Thank you," I say. "But I'm just Average Boy—your average, everyday superhero."

She smiles as I turn to leave the room.

"Just think how much more successful your report would've been if you'd read the book," she adds.

Busted. But how did she know I didn't read the book?

Chapter 16

They say time flies when you're having fun. So right now time is dragging like a blanket belonging to a short toddler.

Mrs. Wordsmith gives me a C on my book report. Actually, she gives me an extra week to read the book and give a report that involves my thoughts and ideas from the book. So I do that and she raises my grade to a C. Dad is pretty upset when he sees my initial grade, because he knows I didn't do my best on the project. He's happier with the new grade but says I could still do better. He's always telling me to be a well-rounded kid.

I tell him a C is pretty well-rounded. Not as well-rounded as an O, but an O isn't part of the grading system. Maybe it should be. It could stand for "outstandingly well-rounded."

Anyway, wrestling is over. School is now just classes and homework. I'm currently sitting in math class working on a math problem.

It's 8:05.

Class ends at 8:47.

I'm trying to figure out how many minutes I have until the bell rings. I guess my teacher is right: we do use math in everyday life.

My school doesn't allow us to use our phones to solve math equations during class. So I pull out my phone to text Billy about what we're going to do after school. I'm thinking we could ride over to Mrs. Fox's house and see if she needs help with anything. I love helping people. The fact that Mrs. Fox always bakes us cookies has nothing to do with my desire to help.

I text, "Let's hang out after school. Mrs. Fox probably has cookies!"

Mentioning the cookies isn't the mistake. Baked goods are a big motivation for Billy. Just to make it totally clear, all I want to do is help Mrs. Fox and care nothing about those warm, well-rounded sugar bombs of goodness.

My mistake is not sending it to Billy. I should've

checked, but I am texting under my desk. When I feel my phone vibrate and sneak a peek at my phone, the reply text isn't from Billy. It's from Jackson Billingsley, saying, "Cool. Let's do it!"

Now I'm not saying Jackson is the biggest nerd in school. He's not that tall, so I'd never say that. But let's just say that Jackson thinks it's fun to take a break from reading a history book to do something crazy like read a science book. He's also the type of kid who corrects everyone's grammar and spelling. In fact, if he was reading this right now I'm sure he'd fine somethink to korrect.

You know, if you walked up to Jackson and said, "Can I give you $20?" he would probably say, "The correct way to ask is 'May I give you $20?'" Now that's nerdy!

Not that I would say that. I don't like to say bad things about anyone. Take the Terrible Threesome for example. They are horrible people who love to torture everyone around them. Plus, they smell bad. But I would never say that. I know I'm supposed to love my enemies.

Mark smells the worst of all of them.

Well, maybe I would say it. But I know it wouldn't be very kind if I did. I also know that Jesus loves everyone, and He wants us to do the same. With Jackson, that is quite a challenge.

Speaking of a challenge, our youth group risk challenge is still going. Hanging out with Jackson would be a great way to be a friend to the friendless. Maybe it's a God-thing that I texted Billingsley instead of Billy.

Still, I'm making a mental note to change Jackson's name in my phone so it won't happen again. The only reason I have Jackson's number is because he invited me to his birthday last year. He texted me all the details. I went because Jesus wants us to be kind to others even if they do have free cake and ice cream and a huge bouncy castle at their party.

It was actually a good thing I showed up to his birthday. I was the only one there.

"Let's get this party started!" I yelled, walking into his backyard.

I cut myself a piece of birthday cake and started eating. Then I went over and jumped in the bouncy castle until I got a terrible bellyache. Jackson said I should've done those activities in reverse order. He then suggested that I go home.

As I left the party, Jackson's mom thanked me for coming. She said most of Jackson's friends were from chess club so it was nice meeting someone new. She also mentioned something about the party starting later in the afternoon. I really wasn't paying attention due to my stomachache.

Mrs. Billingsley was being nice to me, so I wanted to do something nice and tell her that Jackson needed to work on not being so nerdy.

"Can I be honest with you, Mrs. Billingsley?" I started to say.

"It's 'May I be honest with you?', Bob." Mrs. Billingsley corrected.

I decided it was a losing battle. I just thanked her for the party and walked home.

Now Jackson thinks I want to hang out with him again. For the rest of math class, I think about how Jackson didn't have any friends at his party. When the bell rings, I text Jackson to meet me at the bike rack after school.

He's right on time. And here's the thing: We actually have fun.

Mrs. Fox makes the best cookies in the world. We sit around, play cards, and eat cookies. Jackson's the best at games. I win at eating cookies. It's strange how I get a bellyache when I hang out with Jackson. I help Mrs. Fox do the vacuuming and wash some dishes. Jackson helps her with her taxes.

When it's time to leave, Jackson thanks me for hanging out. Then he asks if he can be honest with me.

Oh boy, I think. Here comes the part where he tells me that he wants to do more stuff with me.

"Sure, Jackson," I reply. "You can tell me anything."

"That text I sent you that said 'Cool. Let's do it!' wasn't

meant for you," he says. "I replied to the wrong message in my phone. I thought I was texting Trent about chess club. But I've seen how Jordan, Mark, and Luke have been really mean to you, so I thought you could use a friend. We should do this again sometime."

All I can do is laugh.

After I think about it later that night, I text Jackson and say, "If you ever need someone to play chess with, let me know."

He immediately texts back, "You mean, 'someone with whom to play chess.'"

Yeah, I think I'll just keep doing stuff with Billy.

Chapter 17

Billy and I always come up with the best ideas together. The latest is a game we call, "Ceiling Fan Ball Catch." We invent it right after my dad accidentally loses the power cord to our high-tech Atari video game console.

"I was using the power cord to charge something else," Dad says. "Now I can't find it."

I think he's joking about not being able to find the cord. When I ask him what he was charging, he says, "My sense of peace and quiet." Then he tells us to find something else to do.

That's when "Ceiling Fan Ball Catch" is invented! My dad unwillingly causes a lot of things to be invented by banning us from video games.

The best part of the game is its name. Billy and I don't like confusing names. Earlier this year I got really excited when my gym teacher said we were going to play pickleball. I love pickles! I even showed up with my own jar. Turns out, the game has nothing to do with pickles. You just hit a holey ball with a weird racket. Instead of pickleball, it should be called wiffle mini-tennis.

Anyway, our game involves a ceiling fan and a ball. As you can tell, we came up with the perfect name. To play, you throw a Nerf ball into the blades of a spinning ceiling fan. The blades then shoot the ball randomly around the room. The goal is to catch the ball before it hits the ground.

From the start, we can tell it's a good game. On the first throw, the ball shoots to the left. Billy dives and makes an incredible catch! Then we improve the game by moving the couch.

It's actually Billy's idea to clear furniture out of the way. "Ah tink we . . . ahhhhh . . . should . . . moof da ca-ouch," Billy says, gasping for air after hitting his ribs on the back of the couch.

Once Billy catches his breath, we throw the ball again. This time it flies toward our piano. Not only do I catch it, I play a little tune with my face as it hits against the keys. Billy says it's the only time something "in tune" has come from my mouth.

Some people shouldn't try to be funny.

The game is going great until round twenty-four. The ball hits the ceiling fan and zooms toward the bookshelf. I run after it. That's when my dog, who has decided to hang around me again since wrestling season is over, races into the living room. I trip over him and fly into the bookshelf. More specifically, I land on the third shelf from the bottom and learn something amazing. The bookshelf is not bolted to the wall.

How is the bookshelf not bolted to the wall!?! Did my parents miss the safety training session before I left the hospital? What other danger have I been in because of my parents' carefree, nothing-bolted-down lifestyle?

The bookshelf crashes down over me. Fortunately, we have mainly paperback books, so I'm not injured. I am covered in books, however.

When I open my eyes, I realize our big Bible is laying open across my face.

Billy races over and asks, "Read any good books lately?"

My brain shows it's okay by cranking out a joke. "With this Bible on my face, I guess it nose where I stopped reading."

"I'd like to help you," Billy replies. "But I think it's time for me to book."

"Before you go," I say, "can you act like a librarian's favorite vegetable?"

"How's that?" he says.

"Quiet peas!"

This makes us both laugh. Dad must have heard the commotion because he walks into the living room.

"You destroyed our bookshelf and you're making jokes?" he says. "Help me get the bookshelf put back. Do you realize how dangerous that was? You could've been really hurt!"

I slide the Bible off my face and say, "Sorry Dad. I really only have my shelf to blame."

Dad pauses. Then he fills the room with laughter. My dad has the best laugh. It sort of sounds like a steam engine hit a hyena playing an oboe.

We quickly pick up the bookshelf, and Dad bolts it to the wall. He says it'll be safer this way. But to make the house totally safe, he says he's going to bolt me to the wall, too. He's joking, of course. I hope.

Then he points out that it's getting warmer so we should go outside for the rest of the day. He actually says, "for the rest of the year," but I'm pretty sure he means "day."

Billy and I ride our bikes to his house and come up with the perfect outside game. We turn on his TV, grab the wireless controllers to his game console, go outside, and smash our faces against his living room window.

I'm beating Billy in a racing game when his mom catches us playing. Wow! She has a really loud scream. I guess she didn't expect to see our faces peering into the window like that.

She suggests a fun game called, "cleaning the outside of the window." We do it, but it's not that fun. So now we're trying to think of something else to do.

And I've got a great idea.

Chapter 18

Turns out it isn't the best idea I've ever had. One adult, let's call him "a fireman," says it was pretty dumb. It didn't seem dumb at first. I thought it'd be fun to fly a flag Billy and I made on the flagpole at school.

A few years ago, Billy and I built a clubhouse. It was a private clubhouse, so nobody else was allowed in. To make sure everyone knew not to come in, we made a huge flag that said, "Bob and Billy's Secret Hideout." We also painted "Keep Out" on the front wall. It was awesome.

Well, to be honest, it got boring. We spent the first day making plans on how to keep out other kids. The next day we played hide-and-seek. The third day we left to see why no one was trying to get into our clubhouse.

After that, we let everyone in. It was the right thing to do. Plus, it was much more fun to share something cool with friends. And since the clubhouse wasn't private anymore, we took down the flag. We also painted more letters on the outside wall. Instead of "Keep Out," it said, "Keep Standing Out."

The flag had been sitting in the clubhouse for years, so flying it on the school's flagpole seemed like a good idea. It showed we cared about the Earth by recycling. And I could image kids showing up to school, seeing the "Bob and Billy's Secret Hideout" flag, and thinking we'd taken over.

Now I realize it wasn't a good idea. That's another reason why it's good to have a friend like Billy, someone we can blame bad ideas on. But I'm getting ahead of myself.

To make the plan work, Billy and I had to borrow Mr. Polvado's giant ladder.

Initially, we were just going to use the rope and pulley at the bottom of the pole to change out the flags. But Luke overheard Billy and I talking about our plan after school one day and suggested we use a ladder instead.

"That way there won't be any fingerprints," he said.

Luke is way better at being sneaky than us. And the Terrible Threesome have been nice to me lately. And by nice, I mean they have stopped throwing things at me during lunch and gluing the zipper of my backpack shut. All that to say, we actually took Luke's advice.

Mr. Polvado takes a lot of naps. So when we go to borrow his ladder, I didn't want to wake him and ask if we can use it. Later, he thanks me for that. He wasn't actually sleeping, but now he can't get blamed for what happened.

Getting the ladder to school was tricky. I held one end. Billy held the other. That doesn't sound tricky. But when you're riding your bikes, it adds an element of danger.

We quickly discovered to make this work that both of us had to ride at the same speed. Actually, that's what I told Billy as I helped him out of a ditch. I also reminded him that he shouldn't hit the brakes, even if he did see a cool-looking turtle.

We finally got to the school. Then we did the next thing on our carefully planned out adventure. We went back for the flag we forgot. Once we arrived at school again, we got in an argument. Neither of us wanted to climb the ladder.

After about an hour, I said the words that usually get me in trouble.

"Fine. I'll do it."

I wasn't scared. I'm Average Boy! I started climbing like the brave kid God made me to be. Then I realized I forgot to grab the flag.

"I forgot the flag!" I shouted down to Billy. "I'll have to come back down."

"Stop shouting," Billy said. "You're only on the third rung of the ladder. I'll just hand it to you."

Turns out I wasn't as far up as I imagined. Billy handed me the flag and I continued to climb toward the clouds. I needed to hurry so we didn't get caught, so fear couldn't slow me down.

Thirty minutes later something hit my face. My eyes were shut, so I couldn't see what it was. I'm brave but my eyes are little cowards.

I stopped climbing. My face got hit again. My eyes gathered their courage and opened. It was the school flag. I'd made it!

This was when my hands decided to act like my eyes. They clinched tight. I was holding the ladder tighter than my dad held on to the last piece of ham at Christmas.

I was in trouble. Real trouble. I couldn't move.

"This was a terrible idea," I shouted down to Billy. "I'm stuck."

"Hey, that's what the gum said to the shoe," Billy started to joke. But then he saw the terrified look on my face.

He called his dad and told him that I needed help.

The rest of the story isn't that interesting. I'll skip the part where the firemen came, the police put down padded mats, and a fireman climbed another ladder to get me.

In the end I learned an important lesson: Never borrow a ladder without permission.

My parents think that some other lessons are hidden in my little flag raising adventure. For example, they want me to run my ideas by them first to see if they're good ones. Dad reminds me that God gave me parents to help guide me through life.

Mom and Dad also say that they're glad I'm safe. And to make sure I stay safe, I'm grounded for a month. My parents really care about my safety.

But they obviously don't care about me winning the youth group's good-risk challenge. It's hard to stand up for God when you're stuck in the house.

Chapter 19

Easter is always eggs-alent. That's no yolk!

I'm being serious, and not just because I'm not grounded anymore.

Every Easter Mom buys a ton of chocolate eggs and hides them from my dad. On Easter morning my brother and I try to find them before Dad does. It's getting harder and harder. My dad loves chocolate.

Last year, Dad snuck into our rooms and turned off our alarm clocks. We awoke to the sound of crinkling tinfoil and yummy sounds coming from the hallway. Like firefighters on an emergency call—which I now know a little something about—my brother and I jumped out of bed and into action.

Looking back, my brother should've turned off the ceiling fan before jumping from the top bunk. I don't know why he sleeps on the top bunk. He started doing it after I got a water pistol for my birthday. I guess some kids don't like to be prewashed before taking a shower in the morning.

Anyway, my brother staggered into the hallway holding his head. Dad says Brian and I have been blessed with hard heads. Brian showed his toughness by eating one chocolate egg before passing out. Don't worry. The doctor said he'd be fine . . . and that he should probably start sleeping on the bottom bunk.

Our family's rule is that we can eat one chocolate egg before church. This rule started a couple of years ago when my brother devoured eight Cadbury eggs right after he found them. That was also the year we discovered my brother's stomach only holds one Cadbury egg. Once we got to church, Brian made a sick face and out came seven eggs!

Brian ruins everything. At least we still get one egg before putting on our church clothes. Easter is tomorrow, so I'm going to lock my bedroom door, hide my alarm clock, and try to get some sleep.

*

I wake up at 5 a.m. to hunt for Easter eggs. Mom and Dad are already in the living room. My brother and I stumble in with our baskets. Everywhere we look there are eggs. It's like someone scared a bunch of chickens at once. From what I can tell, Dad hasn't taken any. I guess he's still eating healthy.

My eyes are bleary, but I spot an especially large egg hidden on top of the bookshelf. Unfortunately, so does my brother. *This is the real prize,* I think. We eye each other like competing sumo wrestlers. Mom counts us down.

"Three, two, one . . . go!" she says.

I spring into action, diving over the sofa and leaping across the coffee table, which is appropriately named because Dad spills his coffee on it as I bound over him.

Then I notice something strange. My brother hasn't moved. Actually, he's picking up all the other eggs like crazy.

"Aren't you going to go for the big one?" I ask.

"No, you can have it," he says.

He's a really great brother. I start climbing the bookshelf, which is now safe because Dad bolted it to the wall. My brother continues gathering little eggs. That's his loss. This big chocolate egg will last me a whole month!

I keep climbing and grab the egg. Instantly, I know something is wrong.

"What's this?" I shout.

"That's a papier-mâché egg I made in school." Brian grins. "You can have it."

Before I can climb down, my brother runs into his room carrying all the good eggs.

Actually, he doesn't get all the eggs. I find four chocolate eggs that he missed. One is hidden behind a pillow that Dad is leaning against on the couch. He doesn't look too happy that I discovered it.

I'm not happy either. My brother tricked me. Four eggs! That's not enough for even one day. I go to my room and pick out the one egg I can legally eat before church.

The hollow chocolate egg reminds me of Jesus' empty tomb—the real reason we celebrate Easter. And then, a few minutes later, my brother walks into my room and starts piling eggs into my basket.

"Here's your share, Big Bro!" he laughs.

"What do you mean?" I ask.

"Easter is about giving and sharing joy," he says. "I didn't have any money to get you something, so I planted that fake egg so I'd get all the chocolate eggs and could give you half. Happy Easter!"

And it is a happy Easter, until . . . have you ever awakened from a deep sleep and had no idea where you are? That's what happens to me. I feel tapping on my shoulder, startle awake, and shout, "Get away!"

I think that's a reasonable reaction to having a nap interrupted. But it makes the people sitting around me in church jump in their seats. At least Dad stops tapping me.

I love our church's sunrise service. I'd be even more excited about it if the sun rose later in the day. For some reason God made the sun to always rise before 7 a.m. He may never sleep, but that's too early for me.

I spend the rest of the service playing a game I call "trying not to doze off." I lose.

I'm also at a loss as to why we're singing "Shout to the Lord" at 7:18 a.m. At this time in the morning, no one feels like shouting to anyone. Our version sounds more like "Yawn to Yahweh."

Once the service ends, everyone seems happier, especially my dad. The church sets out tables with coffee and

Easter treats. Dad keeps refilling his coffee. I wonder if he's really tired, or if he's doing it so Mom can't smell the chocolate on his breath. He tried to hide it, but I definitely saw him eating the head off a chocolate bunny a couple of minutes ago.

Chapter 20

So far my goal to have an above average year is working out. I'm still in second place for the youth group challenge. At least, I think I am. The youth pastor won't tell us everyone's scores.

Jenny just has to be in the lead. I think she's part Mother Teresa and part Billy Graham. I'm not sure who those people are, but Dad says they did a lot of great things for God.

My youth leader refused to give me credit for the flagpole incident. He said good risks don't involve the police . . . and that my goal during that incident was to lift my name high on the flagpole, not honor God's name.

However, I did get some points for my "Umber Glider." Billy and I invented the Umber Glider, or what's known on the streets as the UGly, on a rainy afternoon. Remember Billy's battery-powered leaf blower? I did. One day I tried to use it to propel myself on my skateboard. It didn't really work. But it had been raining, so I grabbed my umbrella, opened it up in front of me, and turned on the leaf blower. My skateboard started rolling forward! It was like I'd invented a land sailboat. I used duct tape to form the words, "Rolling with God" on my umbrella. Then people would know I loved Jesus . . . and I'd get points at youth group.

Soon tons of kids were leaf blowing around on their skateboards. Gus, who owns the local hardware store, gave my family a $100 store credit because he sold so many battery-powered leaf blowers.

So not only did I share God's love with people, I also helped a local business.

Anyway, spring break is coming and that means I'll be taking another big risk. I'm going on vacation with my family.

Each spring break starts the same way. Dad says a phrase that strikes fear in my heart, "We're off for a fun-filled family vacation!"

Those words may not sound scary to you, but for me they're right up there with, "Look at the sweater your aunt crocheted you!" or "Guess who's turn it is to the clean out the doghouse?" (Spoiler alert: It's always my turn.)

Most families go to fun places like a beach or a rodent-infested theme park. My dad's idea of fun is going to educational places, like old battlefields. We usually stand in an empty field while Dad talks for an hour about what happened there in 1820. This always inspires me to ask patriotic questions such as, "Does our hotel have free wifi?"

This time Dad says spring break will be different. He announces we're going to Fiesta Texas Theme Park!

Instantly I'm skeptical. "Were any battles fought there?" I ask. "Did Santa Anna storm the log ride or something?"

Dad assures me this vacation is all about fun.

"I guarantee you won't learn a thing," he says.

"So it's going to be just like math class," I say.

Dad doesn't laugh. "Go pack your suitcase and get in the car," he says.

For family road trips, we don't take Dad's truck. Instead we all pile into our classic 1996 Lincoln Town Car. If you've never seen this kind of car, just imagine a living room on wheels only bigger.

The great thing about having a car this big is my brother and I can't fight in the backseat. When you have to use walkie-talkies to communicate, it's hard to get into too much trouble.

By the time we pack and explain everything about watching our house to Billy, it's nighttime. Turns out traveling at night is great, because Dad can't see the historical signs. Theoretically, this means fewer stops.

In reality, it doesn't. My mom was born with a hummingbird's bladder instead of a normal human one. That means we always stop a lot.

Every time we pull back on the highway, Dad gives the same pep talk: "Okay, the next exit isn't for another twenty miles. Let's all try to make it."

About eighty-three bathroom stops later, we finally arrive at our destination and start looking for a hotel. My dad is not a man of reservation—or at least he doesn't like to make them.

Maybe because it's spring break or maybe because a new rollercoaster just opened at Fiesta Texas Theme Park, but all the hotels are booked.

All is not lost! Dad remembers a friend who lives closeby. He pulls out his phone and calls Joe, who is on vacation in Hawaii.

"Sure, feel free to stay at my house," I hear Joe say. "There's a spare key hidden in one of those fake-rock things near the back door."

I make a mental note to find out what Joe does for a living. If Joe can afford to go to Hawaii, he must have a great job. Maybe I could be CEO of Joe's company someday.

Hawaii sounds awesome. It's still daylight there when we call, and Joe's kids are surfing.

We find Joe's house but can't find the hidden key-rock. Dad spots a cat door that leads into the house.

"I wonder if that's where the term 'cat burglar' comes from," I say. "If someone was skinny enough, he could fit through that door."

"Remember your joke about being so small you used ChapStick as deodorant?" Dad says. "Let's see if it's true."

To be honest, I didn't think I'd fit at first. But when Mom has to go to the bathroom, she can be very . . . pushy. Soon I'm unlocking the back door. Who knew God could

use my lack of muscles to save my family from sleeping outside?

And once we explain everything to the neighbors and the nice police officers who show up, we're home free. Well, not our home. But it is free.

The only downside of the cops showing up is now I can't get credit for serving my family in the youth group challenge.

For the next three days we have a blast at the theme park. Dad rides the new roller coaster four times.

Plus, we get to see what Dad eats for lunch. It doesn't look like he's eating that healthy anymore.

Once all the food is gone from Joe's refrigerator, we know it's time to leave. We write a nice thank-you note, lock up, and I slip back through the cat door. One hundred and twelve bathroom stops later, we're home.

It's our best family trip yet. No history lessons. No fighting with my brother. Lots of theme-park fun. And I discover I can fit through a cat door.

I guess that means I did learn something.

Chapter 21

I think I have spring fever. Why is it called that? My body
temperature is normal. I just don't want to do school-
work anymore. I don't think that's a sickness; it's normal.
Instead of spring fever, it should be called spring fervor
because I'm so excited for school to end.

I'm also excited about Dylan's slumber party. Of course,
that's another thing I don't understand. Why are these
things called slumber parties? We never slumber. I'm not
even sure how to slumber.

The last time I spent the night at Dylan's house his dad
told us not to stay up too late.

"I'm just here to slumber," I assured him. "Whatever that is."

His dad laughed. But he wasn't laughing the next time he checked on us. And by "checked on," I mean yelled at.

"I told you two not to stay up so late!" he shouted.

"Sorry, Dad," Dylan said. "We're just about to go to sleep."

His dad shook his head. "It's too late for that," he said, taking a sip of his morning coffee.

Sleeping while at Dylan's house obviously isn't a priority, so this weekend should be a blast!

I'm currently preparing my body to stay up all night. By going to bed at 7 o'clock, I'll sleep extra long during the week and build up a sleep reserve. It's very scientific. I should be drifting off to sleep any minute now.

Ever notice when it's time to sleep that your brain decides to start thinking about everything but sleep? Or—and this is super annoying—your brain starts playing back a bad memory that keeps you awake?

Usually praying at bedtime helps me go to sleep, but tonight as I thank God for my new baseball glove, my brain decides to replay my worse baseball memory. It happened last weekend.

Our team doesn't have a lot of equipment. We share

everything, including our batting helmets because our team only has three of them. Our coach must own stock in a company that makes lice shampoo. Everyone on the team has been buying a lot of that lately.

What hasn't happened lately is me getting a hit. But last weekend I finally connected with a pitch. I took off toward first base. My eyes were focused on the base . . . until my helmet (did I mention it was way too big?) swung around and blocked my vision.

The crowd was cheering, so I kept running. Nothing was going to stop me from being safe.

Slam! I hit something and flew backwards into the dirt. Thinking I'd run too far and smashed into the outfield fence or something, I took off my helmet and saw Sarah standing over me. Turns out I didn't run down the first-base line. I ran straight forward and directly into the other team's pitcher.

Sarah apologized for knocking me over. "Looks like you're down and out," she said.

She really needs to work on her apologies . . . and not laughing so loudly.

With that memory over, I finally fall asleep.

When Friday comes, I've stored up plenty of rest. My parents drop me off at Dylan's house at 7, which has become my normal bedtime. Billy, Trent, Mason, and Zander are already there. Dylan says after everyone arrives, we're going to play hide-and-seek outside in the dark.

I'm starting to regret wearing my neon yellow shirt and light-up shoes. But there's no time to rethink my outfit, because the last car pulls into Dylan's driveway.

Oh no! The Terrible Threesome just got out of the car. Why would Dylan ruin his slumber party like this? Jordan looks at me and grins. Is it too late to fake an illness and get my parents to come pick me up?

My parents won't answer their phone, so it looks like I'm stuck. I'm stuck two ways actually. I'm stuck at Dylan's, and I'm stuck in a tree.

Mark is "it." As he counted for the first round of hide-and-seek, I climbed a tree in the front yard. I also borrowed a black hoodie from Dylan, so I'm basically invisible.

I can barely see Mark walking below the tree. There's no way he can find me. As Mark starts to walk away, he stops and looks up.

"I see your flashing shoes, Average Boy." Mark smiles in the darkness. For an evil villain, he sure has white teeth.

"How do you know it's me?" I answer.

"Who else could it be?" Mark says, picking up a rock and throwing it at me.

Mark might have good vision, but he has terrible aim. Instead of hitting me, he hits a limb above me. Let's call it the "owl limb," which is a perfect name because there's a big owl on it.

I didn't even see it sitting above me the whole time!

The owl evidently doesn't like rocks thrown at it. It spreads its wings and swoops down at Mark. As it flies past me, I wonder what kind of owl it is.

I don't wonder long. It's a screech owl. And screech is exactly what Mark does.

He lets out a high-pitched screech, turns to run, and trips over a rock. That's when we both start crying. Mark's crying because he's scared. I'm crying from laughing so hard.

I climb down to make sure Mark's not hurt. He's not, just embarrassed. He begs me not to tell anyone. I make a deal with him. If he, Jordan, and Luke leave me alone the rest of the year, I won't tell anyone about his ability to screech like an owl. He reluctantly agrees.

He also tags me, so I'm the next "it." I'm out of this round of the game, but I feel like a winner.

Mark talks to Jordan and Luke right away. At least I think he does. They don't bother me the rest of the night, which ends up being a blast. We swim in Dylan's pool. We play basketball. Mark even picks me for his team. I may have had something to do with that. As we're picking teams, I say in my best owl imitation, "Who are you going to pick, Mark? Who? Who?"

After the basketball game, we play video games. We never slumber, but I think we're about to go to sleep because we promised Dylan's dad we wouldn't stay up too late.

Uh oh. Dylan's dad just walked in with a cup of coffee. Is it morning already?

Chapter 22

few weeks later, I walk downstairs with a Band-Aid across my nose. The Band-Aid has nothing to do with Dylan's slumber party. Or the owl.

Dylan's slumber party ended on an exciting note. When I walked outside the next morning, that same crazy owl dive-bombed me like I was Mark about to throw another rock. I wasn't holding a rock, just Dylan's pet guinea pig. I guess the owl was looking for breakfast. Or maybe it wanted to nest in my crazy hair. Mom is always saying my hair looks like a big bird's nest.

But let's get back to that Band-Aid. The reason I'm

wearing a Band-Aid is because only one month of school remains, and I'm really trying to make an impact.

"Why do you still have that taped across your face? Your stitches healed days ago," Dad says as I step into the kitchen. "If you want to cover something with a giant Band-Aid, how about your mouth?"

My dad is funny. Maybe my comedy powers *do* come from him.

But he obviously knows nothing about fashion. These days, almost every kid at school is wearing a big Band-Aid on their face.

It started two weeks ago. I can't take all the credit for this cool fashion trend. Billy had a little to do with it. But it really begins with my face.

✳

Billy and I were in the field behind my house bending back tree limbs and letting them go to see how far we could sling pinecones through the air. It's probably how catapults were invented in medieval times.

We were having a lot of fun until Billy let go of a limb while I was standing in front of him.

The limb popped me right in the face. *Whack!* I didn't cry because I'm super tough. However, my eyelids did start sweating like crazy. There was also a whimpering sound, but where it was coming from.

I also had a cut across my nose which I discovered when I wiped my face and looked at my hand. It had blood on it. I'm not sure what happened after that because I decided it might be a good time to take a nap. Being tough can wear you out.

When I woke up, my parents were standing over me. I had to go to the doctor and get stitches. Once the doctor was done, he put a huge Band-Aid over my nose and told me to keep it there for five days.

At first I panicked. How could I show up at school with my face covered by a Band-Aid? I had a reputation to protect. Kids would make fun of me if I looked like a discount mummy. But I tried to stay positive. Maybe it wasn't *that* noticeable.

When I woke up for school the next day and peeked in a mirror, it looked like I had a sleeping bag taped across my face. The tip of my nose was sticking out like it was napping inside. This was bad, so I did what any other superhero would do when encountering a major challenge: I faked an illness. I'd seen movies in which kids pretended they had a fever by holding a thermometer against a lamp, making the reading much warmer.

"Mom, I'm not feeling well," I said when she walked in the room.

Mom responded like she always does. "Let's take your temperature," she said.

She brought me the thermometer. "Your room's a mess," she said. "Maybe all the germs from your dirty clothes are making you sick."

She put the thermometer in my mouth and started picking up clothes. I decided to help by shooting socks into the laundry basket. The Band-Aid must've affected my aim, however, because I bounced a sockball off her head.

Instead of getting mad, she laughed and said, "Blocked! You can't score against me."

Mom bent down to get the sock, and a dozen others that had somehow missed their mark, which gave me time to put the thermometer under the lamp. She kept cleaning, so I kept holding the thermometer to the lightbulb. I was aiming for a temperature of 101 degrees. Every kid knows that's the magic temperature to get a day off of school.

Just before Mom turned around, I shoved the thermometer back in my mouth and let out a yelp. It was really hot!

Mom walked over, took the thermometer from my mouth, looked at it, and said, "Wow, you have a temperature of 128! I'm going to get some bacon strips for your forehead. You can help me cook breakfast before you go to school. Just lay flat."

My plan was obviously ruined. I called Billy and told him I had to go to school with a gigantic Band-Aid on my face.

"Everyone's going to make fun of me," I said.

I walked through the school's glass doors with a hoodie tied tightly around my face. I went straight to my locker, avoiding eye contact with everyone. Billy and Sarah were waiting for me. Billy started laughing. If my best friend couldn't keep from laughing at me, I knew this day was going to be worse than I thought.

I pulled the hoodie off my head and said, "Okay, yeah, I have a huge Band-Aid over my—"

I stopped talking. Billy and Sarah also had Band-Aids across their faces. I looked over at Mason and Zander. They were also putting Band-Aids over their noses.

Turns out Billy got to school early and passed out big Band-Aids. He told everyone it was the latest fashion trend in Paris. Once Sarah stuck one to her face, all the other kids followed along.

Just then, Trent walked by with the biggest Band-Aid I'd ever seen on his face.

"Hey, Average Boy," he said. "I see you belong to the Band-Aid brigade as well. Cool."

What? We even had a name! This was awesome. I quietly thanked Billy, grabbed my books, and headed to math class.

On my way, I passed Mr. Gribble. He turned around with a big Band-Aid over his nose. He gave me a wink and held out his mop, which also had a Band-Aid around its handle.

I had thought the day would be horrible, but it was the best. The rest of the week was perfect too. Well, almost perfect. After a few days, the Terrible Threesome decided it'd be funny to rip Band-Aids off kids' faces and say, "You just got ripped off!"

Some kids just don't know what's funny.

A couple days later, I'm talking to Dad, explaining how the Band-Aid brigade began, thanks to me . . . and a little bit of Billy. And how wearing Band-Aids is currently the cool thing to do.

He nods and says, "That just shows how much power you have to influence people around you, which is why picking good friends is important. Billy and Sarah are good friends."

That gives me an idea. And it has nothing to do with the fact that Dad adds, "You know years ago, some football players would write Bible verses on Band-Aids that they had on their faces. Then the other team and fans who saw them on TV would know they were Christians and get interested in the Bible verses."

I pull two small Band-Aids out of the box. On one I write, "John 3:16." On the other, I put "Joshua 1:9." I stick them under my eyes. Now my face advertises God's truth.

I jump on my bike ready to head to school to be a good influence. My youth pastor is going to love this story.

He just may not like what happens next.

Chapter 23

As soon as I get off my bike, I'm already being a good influence.

"I like the Bible verses," Sarah says.

Mr. Gribble gives me a thumbs-up.

"Great idea," Jenny says with a smile. "I should've thought of that."

Seeing Band-Aids all over other students' faces is a great reminder of how one person can cause big changes. I know I'm being a good example . . . until history class.

That's when Donny walks in the room and I bust out laughing.

Not only does Donny have a Band-Aid over his nose, there's one on his chin and two over his ears. He's obviously trying to become king of the Band-Aid brigade.

Donny greets me with his usual warmth. "Shut up or I'll turn Average Boy into Flat Stanley."

His threat makes my uncontrollable laughter go away. Then Trent walks in and causes it to come back again.

"Donny, did you have a fight with a weed eater?" Trent jokes.

Donny rips the Band-Aids off his face. He's angry. He's also covered in zits. I guess with the ability to grow facial hair also comes the problem of pimples. The Band-Aids had covered many of them up. Now I'm stuck hiding several jokes that I really want to unveil to the class:

"You probably hated that large pimple on your chin . . . until it grew on you!"

"Those pimples make you cool. Now you can be part of pop culture!"

"You'd think it'd be easy to get rid of zits, but there's no pimple way to do it."

So many potential jokes! I sit there thinking about what Donny might do to me if I tell one. I'm just about to say the first one, when I remember what my youth pastor once said: "You have a choice—to lift yourself up by getting a laugh or to lift up God." So I know what God wants me to do.

But then I hear someone else talking. "I'm also done with these Band-Aids, Donny. They're making my face break out. Time to end the Band-Aid brigade."

Donny smiles, and the rest of the kids instantly rip off their Band-Aids. It's the right move.

I'm not bragging, because I didn't say it. After Sarah finishes her comment, she walks over, peels off her Band-Aid, and throws it in the trash. Everyone else follows.

I sit there feeling like I've missed an opportunity. But instead of bringing me down, it fires me up. Like my dad told me, I need to be a good influencer and take advantage of opportunities to do what God created me to do.

I remove my nose Band-Aid, but leave on my Bible verse ones. I want to be a good influence. Plus, they make me look kind of tough.

During lunch I apologize to Donny for laughing at him. He's not mad anymore. I'm feeling so tough and he's in such a good mood that I decide to tell him some of the zit jokes I thought of in history class. Donny enjoys them so much that he laughs and punches me in my arm.

Okay, he doesn't laugh, but he does punch my arm.

I spend the rest of lunch icing down my arm with a cold yogurt cup and plotting a way to be a good influence in my school. Right before the bell rings, inspiration hits me!

Actually, a paper ball hits me . . . right in the head.

But it gives me a great idea. I just need to find some time to talk to the principal.

It's amazing how God makes things work out. I get to talk to the principal during PE.

I start gym class playing Frisbee baseball. But as I run around second base, Jordan hits me in the back of the head with a Frisbee. In total control of my anger, I pick up the Frisbee and begin to calmly inform Jordan that you're not supposed to hit other players with the Frisbee.

Well, that's what I wish had happened. What actually happens is I stop running, pick up the Frisbee, and throw it at him. That sets off a chain reaction of events.

First, I discover I'm not good at aiming a Frisbee. I don't hit Jordan. I hit Jackson. It would have been an amazing throw if I'd been aiming at Jackson, because he is out in left field trying to catch a grasshopper.

Second, I feel bad when I see the Frisbee whack Jackson and he crumples to the ground. (On the bright side, I do free the grasshopper that Jackson has caught.) A second later, he raises his hand and says, "I'm okay."

Third, our PE teacher sends me and Jordan to the principal's office.

My principal greets me with her usual, "What now?"

Jordan and I tell her what happened. We both apologize. She tells us to get along better and get back to PE.

"I'll try to be nicer," I say, "even if Jordan is a terrible person."

Jordan starts to say something but changes his mind and leaves her office. That gives me the opportunity to share my great idea with the principal, an idea that has been taking shape ever since my youth group leader started talking about taking risks for God this year.

My idea is to organize an event at school that raises money for the local homeless shelter. I explain how we could hold a paper toss competition in the gym. Students would get sponsors to donate money so they could compete. Trash cans would be set up at different distances. The competitors would win prizes based on how far they throw and how many paper balls they make in the trash cans.

"We could have it on a Saturday when the gym isn't being used," I say. "I'm sure my youth group could help out. And I could get the chess club to sponsor it. They're probably not good at throwing things, but Jackson and I are friends. At least we were until about fifteen minutes ago."

My principal stares at me blankly. She does that a lot. Then she takes off her glasses and grins. She's on board.

Three weeks later our gym is filled with kids and parents. Mr. Gribble helps set up the trash cans and mark the floor where competitors stand to toss the paper balls.

Workers from the homeless shelter show up to take donations and hand out flyers. My youth pastor acts as the
referee. Jackson and his chess club friends keep score.

The homeless shelter wins big. They end up with more
than $1,000 of donations. Donny wins the actual com-
petition because he throws the farthest. It helps to have
biceps on top of your biceps. Sarah gets second. I'm not
surprised, because she's the best pitcher at our school.

Gus from the hardware store donates a cool headlamp
for first prize. Sarah wins a school shirt for second place.

As we clean up the gym, my youth pastor walks up and
says, "This is exactly the kind of risky thing I was talking
about at the beginning of the school year. How'd you come
up with this idea?"

I can't take all the credit. Whoever threw that paper ball
at me during lunch deserves some of it. However, there's
no way I can know who that was. "Sometimes inspiration
hits me out of nowhere," I say.

I smile. "Right in the head."

Chapter 24

I can tell the school year is almost over because the teachers are showing movies in class. Don't get me wrong, they're very educational movies.

Mr. Garner shows us a history movie. It's about two princesses who have to save their frozen country. Back then princesses sometimes had to marry a person they didn't love to help with foreign relations. In this movie, Anna gets tricked by an evil prince. Fortunately, she and her friend, Kristoff, find her lost sister, Elsa, who saves the country.

When the movie ends, I flip on the lights and Mr. Garner wakes up.

"What's the educational lesson we're supposed to learn from this movie?" I ask.

Mr. Garner thinks for a second. "Over and over, history teaches us it's always good to . . . uh, have friends to help us in life's journey," he says.

"I agree," I say. "Over summer break, I'll try to make friends with a singing snowman."

Speaking of Mr. Garner, as our final test of the year, he gives us the same test that he gave at the start of the year. He says if he did his job correctly, then we'll know all the answers.

He must have done his job, because I ace it! It just goes to show that if you pay attention and then study those quizzes you've stuffed in your backpack all year, then you really do know all the answers.

In art class, Mr. Quick's final "Quick Draw" assignment is to draw something that we want to do during summer. I draw myself leaving school. He looks at the drawing and laughs.

"But it's missing something," he says.

He takes my paper and draws himself leaving the building as well.

All in all, it's been a great school year. I've taken some big risks for God, including trying to make new friends.

Speaking of the Terrible Threesome, they're being not-so terrible . . . at least, recently. It does help that any time Mark starts to get mean, I make owl noises to remind him to "give a hoot, don't be impoloot." (Yeah, I know that should say "impolite," but that word doesn't rhyme and Jackson isn't around to correct me.)

Only one day of school remains. All the tests are turned in, so all that's left is for me to give my teachers gifts and ask if they'll bump up my final grade a bit. You know, the usual end-of-the-year routine. We also have a huge school assembly where the best students receive awards. I usually think of this assembly as nap time.

Wow, it turns out I'm leaving the building with several awards this year. Sarah won so many that she asks me to help carry them for her. It feels great, because I haven't won a school award in two years.

Actually, I didn't even get that award. My elementary school always gave a perfect attendance award if you never missed a day of school. This was before I'd learned the lamp-thermometer trick so I didn't miss any days that year. Since I knew I'd already earned that award, I thought I'd skip the last day as a joke.

Sure enough, Mrs. Dunahoe, the principal, called out my name at the assembly.

"For perfect attendance, we have Bob Smiley," she said. "Congratulations, you weren't absent all year. Bob? Bob? Bob, are you here?"

"He's absent," Billy shouted.

Everybody in the assembly laughed. I wish I could've seen it. Billy said it was the biggest laugh I've ever gotten.

Sometimes I'm not sure if comedy is worth all the sacrifices. I lost the attendance prize and also got in trouble with Dad when he found out that I skipped school. On the bright side, my parents had just bought a new printer, so I made my own award certificates. I gave myself "Best Average Student," "Most Funniest," and "All-Around Average Superhero." I should've won more, but the printer ran out of ink.

The last day of school is always my favorite. I sometimes

feel like an archeologist digging through layers of stuff in my locker. Usually I find an assignment or two that I forgot to turn in. My teachers are always happy for me, but it never seems to change my grade.

This year I don't discover any missing homework, but I do uncover another copy of my Christmas CD. Since it's the last day, I'm feeling generous, and decide to leave it for the next student who gets my locker.

All that's left now is for the bell to ring, so I can rush outside and into the freedom of summer vacation.

Ouch!

Why does Mr. Gribble clean the glass doors in the front of the school so well? He needs to take a little less pride in his work.

My plan to burst out of the school doors is a bust, but our nurse, Mrs. Black, says my busted lip makes me look rugged.

"And I'm really glad to see that bruise on your upper lip has gone away," she says.

"You mean my mustache from the first day of school," I correct her.

She just stares at me blankly.

"It's been a great year, Mrs. Black. See you in the fall," I say.

I speed walk out of the nurse's office, through the tricky glass doors, and toward the bike rack. It may be just the first day of summer break, but I have big plans up my sleeve.

Actually, the paper that my plans were written on kept falling out of my sleeve. I don't know why you're supposed to keep clever things "up your sleeve." So now my plans are currently safely in my backpack, along with all my tests from this year. If you're going to take your school career seriously, you have to learn how to save and organize important papers.

Anyway, my plans include an entire summer of doing things that force me out of my comfort zone to spread God's love.

The first thing on my list is the scariest. And I need to do it now—before everyone leaves for summer break. I'm going to invite the Terrible Threesome to my church. I wanted to do it earlier in the year, but I was too nervous. Now I see Mark, Luke, and Jordan standing at the bike rack.

This game console better be worth it.

Chapter 25

The Terrible Threesome looks like a trio of evil movie villains. I approach them like a Hollywood superhero going into the ultimate battle. My mind may be playing tricks on me, but I feel like I'm moving in slow motion. Even though everything feels like it's moving slowly, I wish I could walk more slowly. I need more time to think about the right way to invite them to church . . . like an extra year.

"If it isn't well-below Average Boy," Jordan says. "Why are you walking so slowly?"

"It's for dramatic effect," I say.

Luke stares at me blankly. "How about this for drama?" he says as he walks by and bumps my shoulder.

"Thanks. I had an itch on that shoulder," I joke.

"Do you have an itch on your face?" Jordan says. "I'd be happy to scratch that for you."

This actually makes me laugh. Donny's always been my biggest bully, so I'm not used to bullies being so quick-witted.

"My face is itch-free," I assure him. "Speaking of free, would you like some free pizza?"

"Oh, so you want a pizza me?" Mark says.

I don't want a piece of him. I'm a joker, not a fighter. But he's smiling at his "piece of me" joke, which gives me courage.

I laugh and say, "I'm being serious. You guys can have free pizza and an owl's favorite drink."

The mention of an owl makes Mark stop smiling.

"What's an owl's favorite drink?" Jordan asks.

"Hoot beer."

All three of them bust out laughing. They quickly try to stop when they remember they're supposed to be acting like mean bullies. But I continue, "At least I think that's what owls drink at their special prison." I pause for dramatic effect. "You know, Owlcatraz," I say laughing, just in case they don't.

They do. And before I can hit them with a joke about an owl's favorite subject in school (it's owl-gebra), Mark changes the subject back to pizza.

"Where do we get this free pizza?" he says.

This is the opening I'm waiting for! My church is having an end-of-school party tonight. I tell them all about it.

"You guys want to come?" I ask.

"Church?" Luke says. "No way. Why would we go to church?"

"Have you ever been?" I ask. "It's fun. And tonight's going to be a big party with games. A lot of kids from school will be there."

After a long pause, I discover none of them have been to church. Turns out, no one's ever invited them.

"Okay, I'll go," Mark finally says, "as long as you stop telling owl jokes."

I agree, saying, "I really don't give a hoot about owl jokes, so I'll see you tonight."

I can't believe it! I jump on my bike to ride home, and I'm definitely not moving in slow motion anymore. I feel like I'm flying. It's amazing how taking a risk for God can be scary but can also feel really great afterwards. Now I just need to let my youth pastor know the Terrible Threesome is coming. He needs to be prepared . . . to give me tons of bonus points for the year-long risky challenge. Jenny might not have the video game console wrapped up yet.

*

I show up early to church. My youth pastor already knows
the Terrible Threesome is coming, because Sarah and Billy
told him.

"It's great you invited them," he says. "But maybe you
shouldn't call them the Terrible Threesome."

"You haven't met them yet," I remind him. "Let's wait
to rename them until the night is over."

I help set up tables and organize the pizza boxes according to topping. For some reason, the youth pastor orders
two veggie pizzas. By the time I get to V, there's no room
on the pizza table so I put them in the church refrigerator.
Nobody here is going to eat those, I think.

I'm setting up some games when the Terrible Threesome
shows up. They're obviously excited to hang out with me
and grow closer to God. I can tell by Luke's first words,
"Where's the free pizza?"

I point to the table. "It's in alphabetical order."

They help themselves. So do a lot of kids from school.
Even Donny comes.

We eat tons. My youth pastor digs the vegetable pizzas
out of the fridge. Somehow those get eaten too. I entertain
everybody by doing my famous trick where I spray soda
out of my nose.

It's an easy trick really. I just need a glass of soda and

someone to say something really funny while I'm taking a sip. That's usually where Billy comes in.

Luke, Mark, and Jordan seem like they're having a great time. After we eat, we play basketball. I let them win. I do this by playing on the other team. Donny, Billy, and I are teammates. I thought Donny would be better, since he's so big. But every time Donny gets the ball, Mark says "eclipse it!" Then Donny bursts out laughing, and Mark steals the ball. Must be the only joke Donny ever understood.

Billy isn't playing his usual good game either. He's afraid I still have soda in my nose, so he won't get anywhere near me. He shouldn't have worn his favorite white shirt tonight. I don't care about losing. I just want the Terrib—uh, those three guys to have a great time. And it looks like they are.

At the end of the night, my youth leader reads some Bible verses about God's love being for all of us. He reminds us that Jesus offers the free gift of forgiveness and eternal life to everybody who believes. It's our job to show love to other people and try to make this world a better place. Then he gives examples of several people in youth group—mainly Jenny—who have taken some cool risks this year and made a difference for God.

Mark, Jordan, and Luke listen to the whole thing. Afterwards, Mark walks up to me and says, "I didn't realize all the good things your church was doing without anyone knowing about it."

"Well, the people we helped knew," I say.

He smiles. "I'm going to go talk with your youth leader."

Okay, until tonight I was having a slightly above average year. Now it jumps up to way above average! Mark has a really long talk with my youth pastor. Then he asks if we can talk privately.

"I guess Jordan, Luke, and I have been huge jerks all year, huh?" he says.

"Come on, let's be honest," I reply. "You guys aren't that huge. But maybe the jerk part is right."

Then he does something completely shocking. He apologizes! He says he'll talk to Luke and Jordan too.

"I promise things will be different when you see us next year," he says.

"Why wait for next year?" I answer. "You can come back to church next Sunday."

"Actually, tonight was fun," Mark says. "I hadn't heard all that stuff about God and doing good things before. I don't know about Luke and Jordan, but I'll be back."

Wow! Things can change quickly. My year just went from way above average to super way above average.

"And thanks, AB, for not telling anyone about the owl—" Mark starts to say, but just then my dad walks up.

"Owls?" Dad interrupts. "Have you heard about the special owl prison called Owlcatraz?"

Mark rolls his eyes and says, "So that's where you get it."

"Like feather, like son," I reply.

Chapter 26

Summer is in full swing! In fact, I'm swinging right now. Billy and I hung a rope from the big tree in our backyard to swing on. It's the perfect length to swing from the picnic table and into the open sky.

Well, now it's the perfect length. When we first tied up the rope, it was too long. Instead of flying into the air, Billy flew into the ground. It's good to have a best friend who's willing to test out your inventions. After we made some adjustments, it was perfect.

My family is taking a road trip to New Mexico today. We planned to leave at 9 a.m. on the dot. Then the dot got moved to 11:30, and it's still moving.

I woke up early to pack the car, so I'd have time to swing on the rope with Billy before we left. Even though our car is big enough to have its own zip code, Dad says I crammed in too much stuff. He makes me leave a lot of essentials I needed for the trip. My pogo-stick goes back in the garage. The miniature foosball table is also a no-go.

We finally hit the road at 1 p.m. on the dot. Dad says driving to New Mexico is a great opportunity to look out the window and view God's greatest creations. I'm excited, mostly because I have lots of movies to watch on my iPad.

We make it almost twenty minutes before Mom has to go to the bathroom. We stop in one of those little towns where the gas station doubles as the general store. Because my bladder is a normal, human-sized one, I take the time to look at the sale table.

Almost immediately, I spot the deal of a lifetime. A slide flute for just one dollar! I had to leave my finger cymbals in the band room at school, so this gives me another musical instrument to master. Plus, it's something to do if my iPad runs out of battery.

I make the purchase, put the slide flute in my pocket, and get back into the car. If you don't know what a slide flute is, imagine a cat getting its tail slammed in your car door. The noise your cat makes is what a slide flute sounds like. It's awesome!

Anyway, the next eight hours of driving are pretty

boring. Dad wants to play some road-trip games. He obviously isn't into the movie I'm trying to watch.

We start with the alphabet game where each of us tries to find the letters from A to Z on car license plates or billboards. Mom wins, and the rest of my movie is actually pretty good.

Next, we play a game where Dad thinks of an animal, food, or place and we try to guess it by asking questions.

I ask my first question. "What is it?"

Evidently, that's against the rules. My brother and I aren't good at this game. Plus, we keep stopping at gas stations and forget the questions we've already asked.

We also try playing the quiet game. I try to be super quiet, but nobody seems to notice. Finally, I say, "I'm really good at being quiet."

"Bob loses," Dad says. "Let's start again."

I use some of the quiet time to think about ways to take good risks for God. Since I'm probably not going to see anyone I meet in New Mexico again, I'm going to try to be bold about sharing God's Word. I've memorized some of my favorite Bible verses, and I plan to tell them to everyone in New Mexico. It'll be great to show so much courage . . . and to beat Jenny.

I'm not sure what she's doing for the risky challenge. Her family went on a short-term mission trip to help out at orphanages in Costa Rica and Honduras. She hasn't checked in with our youth pastor, so I keep winning the vote every week. Of course, I did have to stop wearing those Band-Aids with Bible verses on them because I got a rash.

At 10:30 p.m., the car is totally quiet. I'm not sure who's winning the quiet game—maybe we all won—or where we are. Maybe somewhere in the desert. Mom and Brian are asleep. We all gave up guessing Dad's animal hours ago, and my iPad battery just died. You know what that means. It's slide flute time.

I pull the slide flute out of my pocket and give it a huge blast. Dad quickly pulls over the car. And by "pull over," I mean he hits the brakes, spins the car around on the highway, and ends up in a ditch.

"What was that?" he shouts.

Everyone quickly wakes up. Everyone in New Mexico that is. My dad has a loud voice.

Mom jolts out of her sleep and exclaims, "I think there's a cat with its tail caught in the door!"

"It's my slide flute," I say, showing them my new purchase.

Mom doesn't seem excited that I found such a great deal. Dad isn't happy either, even though nobody's hurt and the car's fine. He says we all need a break.

Brian and I decide to walk up a nearby hill. I learned in science class that rattlesnakes sleep at night, or maybe it was during the day. Either way, the stars look awesome. I've never seen so many of them.

I take the opportunity to try out one of my newly memorized Bible verses on Brian.

"Did you know Psalm 19:1 says: 'The heavens declare the glory of God; the skies proclaim the work of his hands,'?" I quote.

"I did know that," Brian says. "You kept repeating that verse over and over earlier in the day. But it is the perfect verse for right now."

My dad was right about viewing some of God's greatest creations on this trip. To think, we would've missed it. Thank goodness for my slide flute.

After the brief break of looking at the stars, Dad unlocks the doors and lets us back in. The car is out of the ditch and facing the right way. We pull onto the highway and head to the hotel. At least, I hope it's a hotel. I've grown a lot since spring break, so I'm not sure I can fit through a cat door anymore.

Oh, speaking of cats, if you live in New Mexico near highway I-40, you might be able to find a free slide flute laying in a ditch. Just look for the deep swervy tire tracks.

Three hours later, we make it to our hotel. My family is super tired, which most people are at 2 a.m. I go in with my dad to check-in, so I can tell the hotel clerk about God.

But when Dad and I walk in, the hotel clerk is already reading a Bible.

"Good book," I say.

He laughs, "Yes, it's *the* good book."

We check in and go to our room. Everyone collapses into bed. Dad shuts off the lights and says, "I don't want to hear a sound until at least 9 o'clock."

Twenty minutes later, I still can't sleep. Then it hits me. "It's an aardvark!" I shout.

Dad sits up and turns on the lamp. He looks worn out. But he lets out a big sigh and smiles. "Yes, that was my animal," he says. "Now go to sleep. We'll start the game again tomorrow . . . uh . . . later today."

This trip turns out awesome. We ride go-carts, play putt-putt golf, visit Native American ruins, and eat some of the spiciest food I've ever tasted.

I tell everyone I meet about how much Jesus loves

people and wants to save them. We even get three free laps at the go-cart track. The guy gives them to us after I promise to stop quoting Bible verses to him.

I can't wait for the rest of summer!

Chapter 27

The big day is almost here! The risky challenge winner gets announced at church. Jenny and I have been battling it out for first place all year. This seems crazy because Jenny doesn't even play video games. It's like she's doing risky things just to share God's love. What's she thinking?

I feel like it's going to be close. Every Sunday our youth pastor tells us the score for that week, but not the total for the year. And he also gives bonus points in addition to votes from other kids. So it's difficult to keep track of who's winning overall. Sarah said I could've been using math to keep track of it. But that's just silly.

With Jenny out of the country, I've been getting a lot of votes lately. All that witnessing in New Mexico added up. And last week I organized a "Swap Clean-Up." Families from our church and around town met in the church parking lot on Saturday with things they no longer needed. Then they swapped items with each other for things they might want. Some staff members from the women's shelter showed up to take anything that wasn't swapped. The leftover stuff no one wanted, or "my stuff," as Dad called it, was taken to the dump.

The youth pastor said it was a great way to bring the town together and help clean up yards and houses. I discovered it was a great way to get a raccoon hat. I swapped my old baseball bat for Mr. Polvado's raccoon hat. It had a bit of an odor but Mom said I could wear it inside the house once I was old enough to buy my own house.

On the big day, I arrive at church early. Mom says it's the most excited she's seen me about going to youth group. Surprisingly, Jenny's there. I didn't realize she was back from her mission trip. I gather my courage and ask the question I've been wanting to know all year.

"Why are you trying to win a game console when you don't even play video games?" I say.

She starts to answer, but the youth pastor walks into

the room and announces, "Today's the day you've all been waiting for, at least, I know you've been waiting for it, Bob."

I take a seat and listen to the youth pastor talk about why he challenged us to do risky things and step out for God all year. I'm sure he says a lot of other good stuff, but I'm just thinking about how great it'd be to win the GameStation 6.5.

"So after using math to calculate all the votes, the winner is . . . Bob!"

I'm not sure if my youth pastor says it with an exclamation point, but that's the way I hear it. I can't believe I won! I mean, I can, but Jenny was winning for so much of the year. I look at Jenny. She mouths, "Good job" at me, but there are tears in her eyes.

I start to feel bad. Then I think about all the fun Billy and I—and all my new cool friends—will have. Being a good sport, I walk over and tell Jenny she did some really inspiring things this year.

"Thanks," she says. "But I'm going to do the hardest thing after church. I have to go tell the kids at the women's shelter that I didn't win the video console for them."

Now I realize why she was doing it. Those kids have been through a lot. A video game console would really raise their spirits.

That gives me an idea. I know what I need to do, but I have to ask my dad first.

"Don't go to the women's shelter yet," I say. "Meet me there tomorrow around noon. I think I'll have a surprise."

Jenny looks confused . . . or happy. It's hard to tell with girls.

On the way home from church, I ask my dad a question, "Can we donate your old Atari to the women's shelter?"

It's a big ask, but I feel it's the right thing to do. I explain how Jenny was trying to win the new console for the kids.

"Since she didn't win," I say. "It would really make those kids feel good if we donated our old video game system."

Dad pauses. I can tell what he's thinking. The old Atari means a lot to him. Then he says, "If you think that's the best thing to do, then we'll do it."

As soon as we get home, I text Jenny my plans about the Atari. She texts back, "thx." I thought she'd be more excited, but girls do hide their emotions.

Then I unbox the GameStation 6.5. Billy comes over, and we play a few games. The graphics are amazing. Instead of squiggly lines hitting a fuzzy dot, we're driving cool-looking racecars through futuristic worlds with cool cities and moon-filled deserts. It's even better than I imagined! It's so realistic that I lose one game because I stop my car in the desert to check out what looks like a slide flute on the side of the road.

When Billy leaves, I gather up the old Atari. I sit looking at both consoles. Doing risky things for God all year has been the best. I know I've made God happy and helped a lot of people. And now I'm being rewarded for it. I wrap up the console and fall asleep feeling great about myself.

The next day my parents drive me to the women's shelter. Jenny's already there playing Frisbee with the kids. I join in for one throw, but the Frisbee accidentally lands on the roof. Some kids just don't know how to catch.

I go back to the car and grab the big wrapped box. Jenny gathers up all the kids. She still looks disappointed.

I stand next to her as she says, "I know I told you guys I was trying to win a GameStation 6.5," she mutters, giving the kids the bad news. "I really tried all year—"

"And she did it!" I interrupt. "Here you go!"

I hand the wrapped box to a couple of kids sitting up front. They tear off the wrapping paper to reveal the new GameStation 6.5. Jenny stares at me blankly and then starts crying. I thought she'd be happy. I guess you never know what girls are thinking.

Dad walks over and gives me a hug, "I knew you'd do the right thing," he says.

We all run inside to set up the video game system.

It's funny. Yesterday I thought I knew what it felt like to be a winner. But today I know what it feels like to be a real winner.

Jenny comes over and hugs me. "You surprise me sometimes," she says.

"I surprise myself sometimes," I say. "All year I thought I was competing against you, but it looks like we're on the same team after all."

"Speaking of teams, will you be on my team and teach me how to play this video game?" Jenny asks.

A kid from the shelter hands us two controllers. It does feel really good in my hands, even better than I thought it would.

Now if you'll excuse me, the director of the women's shelter just asked me to step outside . . . or put my raccoon hat back in the car.